THE
REDEMPTIVE
TRUTH

THE REDEMPTIVE TRUTH

Releasing Past Pain

A Novel

DR. KETRA L. DAVENPORT-KING

Dedications

To Keenan, Kennedi, and my grandchildren, Za'Drianna and Kingston, thank you for your unconditional love. I am proud to be your mother and grandmother. To my husband, who loves me just as Christ loves the church, you have been my greatest supporter and always allowed me the space to spread my wings as the woman God has called me to *be*.

Special Thanks

To my mother, you are my anchor and strength. Your love and support throughout every part of my life molded me into the woman I am today. To my sister, thank you for being my sounding board for everything! Special thanks to my mentors, beta readers, and friends who continue pushing me to see beyond the shattered glass in my life and share stories that hopefully help others live out their truth. Thank you, Brian; your wisdom is immeasurable.

Credits

To every woman, man, and child who has experienced any abuse, you are FREE in Christ!
Pastor Willie King, Spiritual Contributor
Octavia, MUA, and Photographer – *For Beauty Sake*
Book Cover Design – Rock Dimensional Consulting

CONTENTS

CHAPTER 1

Pastor Douglas Harrington, II sat at the head of a round, polished mahogany table, his presence commanding yet approachable. Unlike his father—who used to hold leadership meetings in his office—Pastor Douglas held his meetings in a conference room where Children's Bible Study classes used to be held. The new conference room reflected his elegant, warm, and meticulously organized personality. The walls were lined with bookshelves, each with an impressive collection of theological texts, history books, and novels. A large, framed portrait of the church's founding members hung above the fireplace, a testament to his father's legacy, the late Bishop Douglas 'Ed' Harrington, Senior, who had dedicated his life to preserving. The mantle was adorned with various accolades and photographs, capturing significant moments in the church's vibrant history.

Sunlight streamed through the large, arched windows that framed one side of the room, casting a gentle glow over the rich, cherry wood furnishings. The room smelled faintly of polished wood and a hint of lavender, likely from the small bouquet of fresh flowers placed in a crystal vase on the desk.

Pastor Doug's stylish casual attire reflected his impeccable taste and the understated elegance he became known for once he embraced his role as Senior Pastor. Even when he spearheaded the bi-weekly leadership meeting, he dressed to impress, and this beautiful summer day was no different. He wore a light, tailored linen suit. His shirt was a soft shade of pale blue, the fabric breathable and perfect for warm weather. The shirt was buttoned neatly to the collar, but he left the top button undone for a relaxed, approachable look. The sleeves were rolled up just below the elbows, revealing his muscular forearms and adding to his casual yet polished appearance.

"Thank you all for adjusting your schedules to accommodate the unexpected change this week," Pastor Doug said. "I tried to rearrange my doctor's appointment. However, he could only fit me in his schedule before going on vacation, which was on our regularly scheduled meeting day."

"That's okay, Pastor. Things happen," said William.

This support from Pastor Doug's older brother would have been non-existent just one year earlier. It was no secret to anyone that William wanted—and felt he deserved—to be their father's successor. He protested, pouted, and, unbeknownst to anyone other than his wife, JoAnn, cried about being passed over.

"Yeah, the change worked out for me, too," said Constance. "I have to run some errands and get some things taken care of today."

"You mean, finally getting that vehicle inspection done on that car," William teased.

"Stay out of grown folk's business," Constance fired back and tossed a peppermint across the table at her brother.

The other leadership team members and Pastor Doug chuckled at the banter. It took close to a year for the newly appointed church leaders to get to the point where playful joking could roam and usher in a joyous mood. The pastor had no desire to cut it short—usually waiting the five to ten minutes it took to fizzle out before starting their meetings.

Pastor Doug facilitated their meeting like an Army General. He wasn't as rigid as General MacArthur, but the team members knew that they needed to make their points and be prepared to defend any views they had that were contrary to the group's position. He listened intently as the event coordinator, youth minister, outreach director, and choir director brought up topics of concern. The agenda covered an array of upcoming events and projects: a community outreach program, the annual Christmas play, a charity fundraiser, and a youth retreat.

"Remember, our goal is not just to bring people to the church but to *bring the church to the people,*" Pastor Doug emphasized, his voice resonating with conviction and warmth. "Let's ensure every event reflects our church's mission and values."

Nods of agreement and murmurs of affirmation circled the table. The team was energized and inspired by their leader's vision and dedication.

"Lastly, we have less than two weeks before our annual turkey giveaway and food pantry outpouring. We've got to be ready to feed folks during the Thanksgiving holiday. Constance, how are we looking in preparation for that?"

"Everything is going as planned. Turkeys are already in. I contracted with the supermarket down the street to keep our turkeys in their deep freezer. We have exactly 100 turkeys ready to be distributed; we did learn last year that not everyone likes turkey for Thanksgiving. This year, we will also have 50 honey baked hams to accommodate the families."

William held up his hand. "I'm one of those folks. Turkey is too dry. Give me a ham any day."

"That's why you've got high blood pressure now," Pastor Doug said, laughing.

3

"Facts," Constance said. "Anyway, we've prepared more pre-made meals that don't include turkey. We'll even have a vegan station. Katherine will be running that section."

"Good. Sounds like you're on top of it."

"I can show you what we've spent," Constance said.

Pastor Doug shook his head. "I don't need to see it…at least not today. I know you're on top of it. We can discuss numbers at the end-of-year budget meeting."

Constance nodded. She appreciated that her brother allowed her to run the event without his micro-management. The previous year, their father put William in charge of the program, and being the micro-manager that he was, a weekly budget meeting was mandated. They argued before, during, and after every session.

As the meeting drew to a close, Pastor Harrington gave each person a moment of individual attention, ensuring they felt valued and understood. William lingered after everyone left to speak to Pastor Doug. After they finished their brief pow-wow, they exited the conference room together—William headed to the parking lot, and Pastor Doug went back to his office.

A sigh escaped his lips as he plopped down in his plush chair. The chair—like every other piece of furniture in the office—was new. He felt his father's furniture had witnessed too many wrongdoings and was somehow tainted. As the full-time Senior Pastor, his message was that it was a new day when he took over as Senior Pastor. That "new day" came with new furniture.

The chair was upholstered in rich, dark brown leather that exuded a subtle sheen, hinting at its high quality. The leather was buttery soft, with deep, cushioned padding that promised hours of comfort. His desk was glass and shaped like a half-moon. Against one wall stood a large oak bookcase, its shelves lined with an impressive array of books and decorative items. The rich, dark wood of the bookcase added to the room's warm ambiance, and its shelves were meticulously organized, reflecting Pastor Doug's attention to detail.

In one corner of the room, a cozy seating area offered a more relaxed setting for informal conversations or quiet contemplation. A deep, forest green leather sofa, plush and inviting, was paired with a matching armchair. A small, intricately carved wooden coffee table sat between them, often holding a pot of freshly brewed tea or coffee and a vase of fresh flowers.

With Christian instrumental music seeping from the surround speakers—one upgrade his father added that he decided not to do away with—Pastor Doug closed his eyes, trying to relax for a few minutes before leaving for the day. But, as was usually the case, there was a knock at his door seconds after his eyelids closed.

"Come in!"

The door opened slowly, and a person he hadn't seen in months stepped in—Constance's ex-husband, Clarence.

"Clarence! What a surprise!"

"Do you have a minute, Pastor? I promise you, this won't take long."

"Of course, I have time for you, brotha."

Pastor Doug walked around the front of his desk and approached Clarence with his arms open wide. Clarence's eyes flickered with a mix of desperation and resolve as he approached the pastor. They hugged for a few seconds, and then the pastor urged him to sit down. Pastor Doug sat on the edge of his desk, flashed his award-winning smile, and folded his arms.

"So, what brings you here?"

Clarence's eyes ping-ponged around the room as if he expected to see someone hiding in the corner or surveillance cameras. He knew the surveillance cameras existed but didn't know where they were placed. He reasoned that it didn't matter. The odds were great that they weren't programmed to record conversations because a pastor discussed too many sensitive things with too many sensitive people—ever to authorize the recording of his meetings.

"Umm, I've been meaning to come talk to you. And since I was in the area, I figured today was as good of a time as any. I've been sitting in the parking lot for a little over an hour. When I arrived, I saw Constance getting out of her car. I didn't expect to see her here today, so I decided it was best that I wait for her to leave."

"Good call. It would not have been good running into your ex-wife. She still has her issues with you," he chuckled. "Due to a scheduling conflict, the church leaders were here because I had to change our weekly meeting." Pastor Doug walked around the table and sat in his chair. Sensing the gravity in Clarence's voice and gaze, he asked, "What's troubling you, Clarence?"

"Well, you may or may not know, but I had an agreement with your dad…Bishop 'Ed' Harrington."

"What kind of agreement?"

"We agreed that if I'd keep the fact that my marriage to Constance was a facade, he would wire a payment of $5,000 a month to keep me quiet."

Pastor Doug's eyes widened, and his eyebrows arched. Clarence's words shocked him like a boxer's stiff jab. He studied Clarence for a few seconds to see if he was joking, but when the frail man didn't crack a smile, Pastor Doug knew this was not a prank.

With a blank stare, pondering on the words he had just heard uttered from Clarence's mouth, he began thinking, *Now…I could throw him out of here, but I don't know who's still lurking in the hallways and might see me. Or, I can pretend I'm interested in his agreement with my father and gently remind him that I'm not my father. Nah, he reminded himself, you are a pastor now, Dougie! You've got to remember to always conduct yourself like one. You can't be throwing people out of buildings and fighting like you used to. It's a new day—time for a new approach.*

Pastor Doug leaned forward and planted his elbows on his desk.

"Clarence, my father never told me about any agreement, but I'm not suggesting you are lying. In fact, I believe you because I know how my father moved—he was not immune to under-the-table deals. But…I am. And I'm sorry to say this, but I can't honor any arrangement you and my father had."

Clarence leaned back in his chair and draped one leg over the other. He looked at his manicured fingernails while he spoke. "Pastor, has Constance come out of the closet to your congregation?"

"No, she hasn't."

"Does the church know that your brother, William, has been sleeping with his students, and it's alleged that during his tenure at the college, at least three former students had gotten pregnant by him, and he paid for their abortions?"

"I wasn't aware of that, so I doubt if any church members know about that to my knowledge. How do you know?"

Clarence held up his hand and cut Pastor Doug off. "Pastor, stop it! Your brother is a lothario. Everybody and their mama knows it. They may not know about the pregnant college girls…but that can change really quickly." Clarence stood up. "I'm sure your congregation doesn't know how for years, your father turned a blind eye and allowed Deacon

7

Harris to molest, abuse, and rape girls—including several members of your family, in particular the one that I was married to. As I stated when I came here…your father and I had a deal, and I expect you to honor it. You can keep paying me five thousand dollars a month or arrange a lump sum payment of one hundred thousand dollars to keep me silent. I'll even sign a non-disclosure agreement."

The room fell silent, the air thick with tension. Pastor Doug felt a bead of sweat form on his temple. "Clarence, let's discuss this rationally. Blackmail is not the answer."

Clarence's eyes hardened. "This is the only answer I have left. I'll be back in 30 days for the money. If not, the truth comes out."

With that, Clarence strutted toward the door, leaving Pastor Harrington stunned. Even his hips seemed more liberated since the divorce and Pastor Ed's death. Before exiting, he tossed one last salvo over his shoulder. "I'd hate to see you lose your new position and your family's reputation be tarnished forever."

After the door closed behind Clarence, Pastor Doug leaned back in his chair and stared at the door. He knew he had to act quickly, but how? His mind raced as he searched for a solution; his family's and church's futures hung in the balance. An answer to this quagmire eluded him, but he did have one prevailing thought. *I should've tossed his narrow butt out of my office before he had a chance to blackmail me.*

Pastor Doug spent the next twenty minutes staring aimlessly at the wall and strumming his fingers on his desk. Suddenly, an idea came to mind as boldly as Clarence had entered his office. He whipped out his cell phone and fired off a text message:

Meet me at Overbrook Park tonight @ 7 pm. No
questions. I'll explain everything when I c u.

He allowed the phone to rest on the desk while he buried his face in the palms of his hands.

No turning back now, Dougie, he thought and allowed a loud sigh to carry away the stress trapped in his lungs.

CHAPTER 2

Dr. Riggio's office was an oasis of calm amidst the hustle and bustle of downtown Chicago. The space exudes a refined elegance, with plush carpeting underfoot, warm, ambient lighting, and floor-to-ceiling windows, offering a panoramic view of the city's skyline. Rich mahogany bookshelves lined with medical texts and classic literature dominate one wall, while tasteful modern art adorns the others, adding a touch of sophistication. The scent of freshly brewed coffee mingled with a faint hint of lavender, creating a welcoming atmosphere.

William Harrington, known to most as Deacon, sat in the client chair—a luxurious, high-backed seat upholstered in soft, dark leather that invites one to relax and open up. He fidgeted slightly, running his fingers along the armrests, his usual confidence seemingly diminished in this setting. At that moment, he wasn't the composed figure he was known to be but a man on the verge of revealing deeply buried truths.

Standing nearly six feet tall in four-inch stilettos, Dr. Riggio struck an opposing figure as she entered her office from a door located in the back of the room. Her demeanor was both regal and presidential. Seeing her bark orders in the Oval Office would not be a stretch of the imagination; she had that type of presence.

"Hello, William."

"Dr. Riggio," William replied, his eyes scanning her curvy figure from head to toe, eventually settling on her muscular calves as she settled in her plush leather chair and crossed one leg over the other. "You're looking as lovely as ever."

Dr. Riggio caught the flirty remark but flicked it away like a pesky fly. She was attractive and knew it. After twenty years of practice, she'd learned to handle flirtatious clients—ignore their advances and then put them on the defensive by peppering them with questions about their behavior. It was the kind of strategy that everyone had employed, from Chess Grandmasters to Super Bowl-winning football coaches—the best defense was a good offense.

While settling in, a notebook and pen were ready, and her eyes locked in on William. Let the games begin.

"William, this is our third session, and I noticed that you do the same thing at the start of each session."

"What's that?"

"You flirt with me when you greet me."

"Who me?" William said, with a sly grin on his face.

"Yes…you. I'm trying to understand why you feel the need to do that. I mean, as a college professor, I'm sure you understand how thin the line between being polite and sexual harassment can be. Therefore, I'd expect you to have a better rein in your tone than most, if not all, of my patients. But you repeatedly straddle the line. Have your flirtatious ways ever gotten you into hot water at the University?"

William's smirk vanished faster than a puddle of water in the middle of Death Valley on a blazing hot summer day. His eyes darted around the room as if an answer to her question might be found. After a few seconds passed, he cleared his throat and let out a strained, "No."

Dr. Riggio nodded and looked at her notes. Round one—Riggio.

"Let's talk about your relationships with women. Although you are married, you've mentioned that committing to one person is difficult. Can you tell me more about that?"

William took a deep breath, his eyes darting momentarily to the window before returning to Dr. Riggio. "It's just...I don't know. Before getting married, I had a pattern of getting close to a woman and then pulling away."

"You must have gotten over that tendency because you eventually married your wife."

William shrugged. "Being from a family like mine, you're expected to get married. Don't get me wrong, I love my wife. But that expectation from my family—especially my dad—made my decision to get married a little easier."

Dr. Riggio nodded while she scribbled notes on her pad. "Often, our adult relationships reflect patterns we've learned in our childhood experiences. You've told me a bit about your father and how he was often absent when you were a child. How do you think his neglect impacted you?"

A flicker of pain crossed William's face. "He was never there. He was always at the church. When he wasn't at the church, he traveled the country as the great and well-known 'PREACHER' at other churches. I'm not sure if you know, but that's how pastors supplement their income, especially in the early stages of their careers when they are at churches that offer low salaries. However, looking back now, I am not sure that is what he was doing," he mumbled under his breath."

Dr. Riggio acknowledged his point with a slight head nod.

"And then, when he wasn't at the church or traveling, he was doing other stuff."

"Like what?"

As William recounted his late father's indiscretions, an ominous feeling seeped into Dr. Riggio's office, subtly altering the previously serene ambiance. The cityscape outside seemed to blur, the vibrant energy of downtown Chicago muted by the weight of William's revelations.

The soft, warm lighting took on a slightly dimmer hue, casting longer shadows that crept across the plush carpeting and the elegant furniture. Once a symbol of sophistication and calm, the art on the walls now appeared to watch over the room with an eerie stillness, their once vibrant colors muted and somber.

William's voice filled the space, low and burdened with the past and his undisclosed trauma.

"My father was supposed to be a man of God. But he…he had affairs, many of them, with women from the congregation. It was like he couldn't stop himself."

Dr. Riggio's expression remained composed, but her eyes displayed a flicker of concern. The comforting scent of lavender and coffee now seemed incongruous, starkly contrasting the dark story unfolding. Despite the pleasant summer day outside, a chill seemed to settle in, as if the room absorbed the gravity of William's words.

"He'd preach about sin and repentance on Sundays," William continued, his voice trembling slightly, "and then spend the nights secretly indulging in the actual things he condemned. My mother knew, I think, but she never spoke of it. And I…I watched it all, pretending it wasn't happening."

Dr. Riggio shifted slightly in her chair, the notepad momentarily forgotten. "That must have been incredibly confusing and painful for you as a child growing up in a house of such contradictions, where the person you loved and looked up to lived a double life."

William nodded, his gaze distant. "It was like living in two worlds. At church, he was this revered figure, respected, and admired. At home, he was a different man, unpredictable, dark, and detached. I guess I learned to hide my true self like him."

The room seemed to close in, the air thick with unspoken pain and long-held secrets. Once a source of light and openness, the floor-to-ceiling windows now felt like barriers, keeping the outside world at bay. The office, once a sanctuary of healing, was momentarily transformed into a confessional, heavy with the weight of past sins and the echoes of a troubled legacy.

Dr. Riggio leaned forward, her voice soft but firm. "William, acknowledging these experiences is crucial. They have profoundly shaped your actions, but they don't have to define who you want to become—that is why you are here, right? We can work through this together, unraveling the past to build a healthier, more authentic present."

As the session continued, the ominous feeling lingered, a silent witness to the pain being unearthed and the tentative steps toward understanding and healing.

"Even when he was alive, he was distant. I just learned not to rely on anyone being there for me for a long time…I became self-reliant and depended on myself and my feelings."

"William, that feeling of neglect can leave a deep mark, making it difficult to trust that someone will stay. Your womanizing habits might be a way to protect yourself from the vulnerability of being hurt again. By not committing, you keep yourself safe from the potential pain of loss or rejection."

"You are right, Doc. I never thought of it that way. I always just felt like… like I was…broken."

"You're not broken," Dr. Riggio assured him. "You're coping with old wounds in the best way you know how. William, the problem is how you cope, which can hurt you, your life, and the lives of the people you love."

William nodded shamefully.

"Recognizing this pattern is the first step toward healing and building healthier relationships, especially with your wife. It's a journey, William, but it is not one that you have to take alone."

CHAPTER 3

When William's wife, JoAnn, entered Dr. Riggio's office, she immediately recognized the wall of books; each time she walked into the office, her breath was taken aback. As an avid reader of romance and autobiographies, she was immersed by how manicured and aligned the books lined up on the shelves. They were medical and psychology-related books, so they weren't her cup of tea, but she was a true bibliophile; therefore, it didn't matter—the perfect alignment of their book spines was enough to feed her addiction.

The office was filled with a faint aroma of freshly brewed coffee. Dr. Riggio, seated across from JoAnn, regarded her with a calm but attentive gaze, a legal pad balanced on one knee, her pen poised and ready.

JoAnn first avoided Dr. Riggio's eyes, focusing on the carpet texture beneath her heels or the small clock ticking softly on the desk behind Dr. Riggio. The rhythmic sound felt like a countdown, each second pulling her closer to a moment she wasn't sure she wanted to face.

"You've been quiet for a while," Dr. Riggio said gently, her voice low and measured. "Take your time, but remember, there's no judgment here. This is your space to be honest."

JoAnn drew in a shaky breath, her chest tight with the weight of words she'd kept locked away for far too long. Since starting counseling with Dr. Riggio, being elusive during their sessions came easy, but today was different. She shifted slightly in her chair, her hands trembling as she finally raised her eyes to meet the doctor's.

"It's…it's not something I ever thought I'd have to talk about," she began, her voice thin and strained. She glanced away again, her gaze drifting to the window where the city outside bustled with life, so far removed from the storm swirling inside her. "Especially not with someone I don't know."

Dr. Riggio nodded, her expression one of patience. "That's understandable. But sometimes, it's easier to share with someone outside the situation. I'm here to listen, JoAnn."

She hesitated, her throat tightening as memories rose unbidden, each a painful shard piercing through her carefully constructed composure. "I don't even know where to start," she whispered.

"Start with what you're feeling right now," Dr. Riggio offered. "What is weighing heavy on your heart today?"

JoAnn's lips parted, but for a moment, no sound came. She took another breath, this one shuddering, and finally, the words tumbled out, fragmented and raw. "I'm carrying something—something I can't tell anyone. Not even William."

William's name got caught in her throat, and she pressed her fingers to her lips as though to push the name back down. But it was too late. Dr. Riggio's pen moved lightly over the page, capturing her words.

"You're speaking about your husband," she said gently.

"Yes," she replied, her voice breaking. "William is everything to me. He is my rock. He is my best friend. And yet…" Her eyes filled with tears she refused to shed, and she looked away, her voice dropping to a whisper. "…I'm lying to him every single day. Yes, we have our share of issues, but deep down, we love each other very much; unfortunately, our past traumas have blurred our present."

Dr. Riggio leaned forward slightly, her presence steady and grounding. "What is it you're lying about, JoAnn?"

She clenched her hands together so tight that her knuckles popped. The question hung in the air like a challenge, daring her to speak the unspeakable. When she finally answered, her words came in a rush, as though she couldn't bear to hold them any longer.

"It's about who I am," she said as she sat still, her voice trembling. "About where I come from. My mother…" she hesitated, swallowing hard before continuing, "my mother had an affair. With Bishop Harrington, William's father."

Dr. Riggio's expression remained neutral, her pen still as she gave JoAnn the space to continue. JoAnn's voice grew softer, the weight of her confession bearing down on her like a crashing wave.

"I didn't know," she said, her tears finally slipping free. "Not until after I married William. I didn't know Bishop Ed Harrington was my father, too."

The room felt heavier, and the quiet was almost deafening as she let the truth settle between them. She looked up, her face etched with pain and guilt. "Do you understand what that means? William is my half-brother!" she shouted.

Her breath harnessed, and she covered her face with her hands, her shoulders shaking as the sobs she'd held back for so long broke free.

Dr. Riggio set her pen down and leaned forward, her voice gentle but firm. "That's a heavy burden, JoAnn," she said. "And it seems like you've carried it for a long time amid everything and everybody, alone."

"*I have,*" she whispered, her hands dropping to her lap as she wiped her tears. "I couldn't tell anyone. Not Pastor Doug, not First Lady

Katherine, and *definitely* not William. It would destroy him. It would destroy everything, our life, our children, our marriage…just everything. Dr. Riggio, I have always felt that Mother Eleanor knows the truth, but she has not said a word to me. Frankly, she doesn't say much of anything to me directly; she communicates everything to William or his brother, Pastor Doug."

Dr. Riggio nodded, her gaze steady. "It sounds like you're trying to protect him and, more importantly, yourself. Living with this secret has taken a toll on you, JoAnn. You have spent years in a marriage with many challenges, including extramarital affairs, secrets, and now this."

JoAnn nodded, her voice barely audible. "Every day, I look at him and feel this crushing guilt. He doesn't know, and I don't know if he ever should."

Dr. Riggio leaned back slightly, her expression thoughtful. "It's clear you care deeply for William and your marriage. But this secret isn't just about him—it's about you. It's not my place to tell you what to do. Your mental well-being and your children are your priorities."

"You and William have some significant things to work through in your marriage. How you choose to do that, JoAnn, will be solely up to you—you do not owe me or anyone an explanation for how you choose to live your life moving forward. Especially given that your trauma has stemmed from past secrets, lies, and deception from one person, Bishop Ed Harrington, unfortunately, who is not alive to face the backlash from his deceit. Remember, life is guided by our choices, security, and finances; consider all three, JoAnn, as you work through this situation between you and William. This will be hard for everyone involved."

Dr. Riggio stood, walked toward JoAnn, and hugged her. JoAnn embraced the hug while settling into the silence between them. Her exhaustion was etched into every line of her face. She stared at the floor, her thoughts swirling, knowing that her truth, once spoken, could never be taken back. But for the first time, she felt the faintest flicker of hope—a small, fragile thing—that perhaps she didn't have to carry this burden anymore.

While JoAnn gathered her belongings, she turned to Dr. Riggio and said, "Thank you. When Pastor Doug required us to begin counseling, I did not know what to expect."

"My journey to coping with my life is far from an end reach, but you have started me toward my personal healing."

CHAPTER 4

Pastor Doug sat on a weathered park bench in Overland Park. The fabric of his black hoodie blended into the growing shadows. The park, usually filled with the laughter of children and the chatter of families, was now almost deserted—the fading sunlight casting long, golden beams across the empty playground and neatly trimmed lawns.

Doug's eyes scanned the park nervously, his hands buried deep in the pockets of his hoodie. He slouched slightly, trying to make himself as inconspicuous as possible. To any passerby, he must have looked like a junkie or a stick-up kid. At that moment, he didn't mind if a civilian mistook him for either. Junkies and thugs were two life forms that civilians avoided like the plague.

The sky was a canvas of orange and pink, the sun slowly sinking below the horizon, casting a serene yet melancholic light over the scene. The distant hum of traffic from the city provided a constant background noise, occasionally punctuated by the chirping of birds settling in for the night.

Doug's thoughts raced as he waited, every rustle of leaves or distant footstep making his heart pound faster. He pulled the hood tighter around his face, shielding himself from the occasional passerby. His mind flashed back to their ten-year stretch on the yard in prison from his drug dealing and gangsta days. It had been over fifteen years since they reconvened. Doug knew that he and Gutter had formed an unlikely bond and that if he needed him, all he had to do was call. They had survived those years together, but their paths had diverged dramatically upon release. Doug had found solace and purpose in faith, while Gutter had continued down a darker path.

Seven o'clock came and went. Doug pulled his left wrist out of the pocket of his hoodie enough to check the time on the cheap wristwatch he wore—it was 7:11 p.m.

"Don't worry, I'm not gonna stand you up," said a voice from the shadows.

Doug flinched and spun around.

A figure approached from the edge of the tree line behind Doug. The figure moved with a casual confidence that belied the tension in the air. Glenn "Gutter" Washington emerged from the shadows, his presence unmistakable. He was a tall, muscular man whose face appeared hardened by years of hardship. He wore a leather jacket, its edges frayed and worn. His walk was a blend of swagger and wariness.

Doug's expression was a mixture of relief and apprehension. "Hey, man…Gutter. Thanks for coming."

"You have been out of the game so long that you dun forgot the most basic rules…never sit with your back to the door, or in this case, to the bushes."

"You're right. You caught me slippin'."

Gutter scanned the surroundings before he extended his fist to Doug, giving his former cellmate a fist bump.

"Just be glad it was me and not one of these wanna be street hustlers." Gutter gestured at the available spot on the park bench. "May I?"

"Please do," Doug said.

Gutter sat down on the bench. "Lookin' good, Rev."

"You too, my man. You're more ripped now than when we were on the yard."

"When we were locked up, staying in shape helped me stay alive. Nowadays, staying in shape helps me feel alive."

"I hear you, my brotha. Well, it's good to see you. What have you been up to?"

"Rev, is that a rhetorical question or do you really wanna know?"

"Rhetorical."

"I thought so." Gutter turned his head slightly to the right and spat. "What you want, man?"

"What…a brotha can't reach out to his old celly?"

"Nig—" Remembering he was talking to a pastor, Gutter caught himself and restructured his sentence. "Bruh, I don't think I've heard from you three times since we got out the *pen*. Matter of fact, this is the first time I've heard from you since you took over your pop's church. And I had to hear about that from my grandmother…you know she's a member."

"Of course, I know that. I see Sista Washington every weekend. Second row on the left—always in the middle of the pew."

"Yep. That's her." Gutter's head turned robotically. He stared deep into Doug's eyes. "What you dun got yourself into that you need me to help you get out of?"

Doug shook his head in disgust and looked off into the distance while he spoke.

"Do you remember when we were locked up, and Johnny Right-Eye was blackmailing Bookie after he caught Bookie tipping into that dude's cell?"

Gutter chuckled. "Yeah…that boy Johnny Right Eye was like J. Edgar Hoover. That fool had dirt on everybody and wasn't scared to use it. That was one crazy white boy."

"He didn't weigh more than a buck-o-five. He needed all the leverage he could get to stay alive. And ole Johnny definitely stayed alive."

"Facts." Gutter smirk dissipated. He watched a few slow passing cars and asked, "Did a Johnny Right-Eye catch you tippin' in somebody's cell?"

"I got a Johnny Right-Eye, but he didn't catch me tipping anywhere. However, he has a lot of dirt on some people I love." Doug looked at his old buddy. "The kind of dirt that could bring down a church and destroy my family's reputation…and please don't ask me what kind of dirt."

"Don't wanna know," Gutter said and waved dismissively. He continued to look off into the distance. "Here's what I do know. I wouldn't be sitting here right now if it wasn't for you. You pulled my coattail when you heard those dudes from 504 Mafia were plotting to lay me down after I beat up that dude in their crew. And when that shady C.O. let 'em in our cell that night, you strapped up and had my back."

Doug nodded slightly and muttered, "Yep."

"We had just become cellys and didn't even know each other that well when that went down."

"Nope."

"I told you back then that I owed you a solid."

"Yep."

Gutter chuckled. "You waited eight years to call it in."

"Better late than never."

"Facts." Gutter looked at Doug. "You wanna see your Johnny Right-Eye again?"

This was the million-dollar question. Doug held Clarence's life in his hands. All he had to do was say the word, and Gutter would see to it that the threats would end permanently. Unfortunately, green-lighting Clarence's death was the only way to know for sure that the threats would stop. As long as Clarence was alive, he'd always have leverage over the Harrington family.

The weight of the situation pressed heavily on him; being seen with Glenn "Gutter" Washington could ruin his hard-won reputation. Yet, desperation had brought him here, and he needed Gutter's help more than ever.

The sun dipped lower, the last light rays casting long shadows across their faces. Doug couldn't hide his angst as the weight of Gutter's question sank in.

"Time is money, Rev. Speak now or forever hold your peace."

"Just scare him."

"Say less." Gutter dug into his jacket pocket and pulled out a phone. "Use this burner to contact me. You know the game…we don't need no record of us talking."

CHAPTER 5

The tiny bistro where Clarence and Malcolm met was a charming, tucked-away gem in the heart of the city. Its warm, inviting ambiance offered a refuge from the bustling streets outside. The bistro's intimate size created a cozy atmosphere, where the soft murmur of conversations mingled with the gentle clinking of cutlery and the occasional hiss of the espresso machine.

Dim, ambient lighting casts a golden glow over the room, reflecting off the polished wooden tables and highlighting the rich, earthy tones of the decor. The walls were adorned with vintage posters and black-and-white photographs, giving the place a nostalgic yet timeless feel. A few potted plants in the corners added a touch of greenery, their leaves gently swaying in the occasional draft from the open door.

The booths, upholstered in deep burgundy leather, provided privacy and comfort. Clarence and Malcolm's booth was nestled in a quiet, dimly lit booth at the back of the cozy corner, partially shielded by a decorative wooden partition. A small, flickering candle in the center of the table cast dancing shadows, adding to the intimate atmosphere.

The aroma of freshly brewed coffee and baked pastries filled the air, mingling with the subtle scent of herbs and spices from the kitchen. The bistro's menu, written in elegant script on a chalkboard behind the counter, offered an array of artisanal sandwiches, soups, and desserts, each crafted with care and attention to detail.

A soft jazz melody played in the background, its soothing notes providing a gentle soundtrack to the conversations unfolding at each table. The bistro's staff moved gracefully between the tables, their movements efficient yet unobtrusive, ensuring that each guest felt attended to without feeling rushed.

Clarence's fingers nervously traced the edge of his coffee cup. Malcolm listened intently, his calm demeanor starkly contrasting Clarence's agitation.

The low hum of conversation and clinking cutlery filled the air, but within their booth, the world seemed to narrow to just the two of them.

"I told Pastor Doug I would go to the press," Clarence said, his voice barely above a whisper, though tinged with defiance. "I threatened to expose all the church's secrets if he didn't pay me."

"Pay you what?"

"Five thousand a month—forever. Or a lump sum payment of one hundred thousand dollars."

Malcolm's eyes widened, but he remained composed, sipping his coffee before responding. "Clarence, do you have any idea what you're getting yourself into?"

Clarence's hand shook slightly as he set down his cup. "Malcolm, I couldn't just stand by anymore without saying one word about that family's deception and long line of secrets…I am at a point of no return with this foolishness! The hypocrisy, the lies…it was eating me alive. They need to be held accountable."

Malcolm reached across the table and placed a steadying hand on Clarence's. "I understand your frustration, but going to the press? You're playing with fire. Those people won't just let you ruin their reputation without a fight. You could be putting your life in serious danger."

Clarence met Malcolm's gaze, his eyes filled with determination and fear. "I can't just do nothing."

"I know, but—"

Clarence held up his hand.

"You don't understand. I've let people take advantage of me and get away with it all my life. Dating back to when I let the first nasty old man—a deacon in that church—raped me. I didn't tell anyone. And then, when I was twelve, my drunk uncle raped me in the bathroom at my grandmother's house during her 70th birthday party. Practically, the whole family was there, and I didn't tell a soul—too scared about what he'd do to me."

"After college, I came back to Chicago and let my family members pressure me into returning to that church and re-experience my trauma all over again."

"Is that when you met Constance?"

"No, I'd known Constance since we were elementary school age. We grew up side-by-side in children and youth church together. I didn't learn that she was a lesbian until I returned here after college."

"How did you find out?"

"We ran into each other at a gay club."

"Which one?"

"Do you remember Club Chameleon? It was on the southside."

"I remember that club. It burnt down, right?"

"Yeah. Electrical fire. Anyway, I was in there chillin', and guess who comes waltzing in there…Bishop Ed Harrington's only daughter, Constance."

"I know she was shocked to see you."

28

"She looked like she'd seen a ghost," Clarence smirked. "I walked over and grabbed her and whispered in her ear, 'Your secret is safe with me. My people don't know about me either.' From that moment, we became the best of friends. We pretended to be dating in public—had all the church folks fooled—and did our separate thing at night."

"What made y'all get married if everything was working smoothly?"

"Her daddy went to the church on a day when he wasn't supposed to come in. He caught her locking lips with a girl."

"At the church?" Malcolm asked in astonishment.

"Yep…at the church."

"Scandalous."

"Very. In fact, because her dad was so afraid that one of the nosey ushers knew about it, he did something about it."

"What?"

"The first thing he did was have that usher kicked out of church for supposedly sliding a few bucks from the collection plate and into her pockets."

"Did she really do that?"

"Who knows? Once the church pastor accuses you of something, it's a wrap—po' thing was out of there faster than she could say her name." Clarence sipped his coffee. "The next thing he did was make Constance marry me so we could stomp out any rumors about her being a lesbian."

"How did he know you were gay?"

Clarence's eyes seemed to turn black. His lips pursed. "He knew because it was his right-hand man who introduced me to gay sex, Deacon Jones."

"He knew you were being molested?"

"That bastard practically sicked that dirty predator on me. Deacon Jones was evil!"

"Oh my God," Malcolm said, reaching for his imaginary necklace.

"Now you see why I can't just let this go. That church owes me, and I intend to milk them for every dollar I can."

Malcolm squeezed Clarence's hand gently. "First, let me say this…I believe every word you just said, and I don't blame you for wanting to get them back. But I've got to ask…is there a safer way to do this? Have you thought about what Pastor Doug might do to keep his father's secrets buried? People like him, they'll stop at nothing to protect their image. You need to think about your safety."

"What should I do, then? Just let them get away with it?"

"*No*," Malcolm replied firmly. "But you need to play this smart. Gather evidence and make sure you have witnesses. You need concrete evidence so it is not your word against his. Do you know what I mean, Clarence? Maybe, consider going through legal channels. Blowing the whistle doesn't have to mean risking your life. We can find a way to expose the truth without putting you in harm's way."

Clarence sighed, the weight of the situation settling heavily on his shoulders. "I just want to make them pay, I have lost a lot behind The Harrington family."

"Is that all you want?" Malcolm asked and then shot Clarence a side-eye.

"I could use the money, too," Clarence replied with a devilish grin.

As they sat, staring at each other, the world outside the bistro continued to buzz with life, oblivious to the high-stakes conversation unfolding within. At that moment, Clarence knew he wasn't alone, and with Malcolm by his side, he felt a renewed sense of hope and determination to face whatever challenges lay ahead.

CHAPTER 6

Constance Harrington stood outside her therapist's office, her hands trembling slightly as she fidgeted. The hallway felt unusually quiet, the air thick with an almost oppressive stillness that seemed to amplify her heart's pounding. The familiar, faint scent of lavender wafted from the nearby waiting area, usually a calming presence, but today, it did nothing to soothe her nerves.

The door to the office loomed before her, a solid, imposing barrier between the world outside and the vulnerable conversation awaiting her inside. Constance's breath hitched as she glanced at the small plaque beside the door—her therapist's name neatly etched in gold letters. She had been here countless times before, but today felt different. The weight of the topic she was about to discuss pressed heavily on her chest, making it hard to breathe.

Her thoughts swirled in a chaotic mix of fear and uncertainty. *What if I can't find the right words? What if I am misunderstood?* She suddenly became conscious of her outfit: snug blue jeans, a short-sleeve collared Polo shirt, and a pair of Jordan Retro 11s. Swaggy? Yes. Feminine? Not by a long shot.

Constance felt a knot tighten in her stomach, her anxiety threatening to overwhelm her. She took a deep, shaky breath, her eyes closing briefly as she tried to steady herself.

The soft hum of the building's ventilation system was the only sound that broke the silence, its rhythmic drone both comforting and unnerving. Constance's pulse quickened as she raised her hand to knock, her knuckles hovering inches from the door. The cool, polished wood felt unyielding beneath her touch as the tumultuous emotions swirled within the pit of her stomach.

As she stood there, poised on the brink of confrontation with her deepest fears, Constance realized that this moment—this decision to step forward—was the first crucial step in her journey to understanding herself. With one last, fortifying breath, she finally let her knuckles rap gently against the door, the sound echoing softly in the hallway. The door opened, and she stepped inside, ready to face the conversation that would forever change how she dealt with her past and future.

"Hello, Dr. Riggio," Constance said as she entered.

Dr. Riggio's head was down, and her eyes were glued to the paper she held. She was so engrossed in her work that she didn't hear Constance knock and was startled when she spoke.

"Constance! It's so good to see you," Dr. Riggio greeted. "Please come in and have a seat."

Constance sat in the chair the doctor directed her to.

"I was just reading an article by a colleague."

"Don't let me interrupt you, Doc. Do your thing."

"You're not interrupting me. I'm almost finished. I can pick up where I left off after our appointment." Dr. Riggio grabbed her notepad and walked over to the high-back chair she sat in during sessions. She draped one leg over the other, thumbed through her notes, and nodded.

"Ahh, we were really making progress during our last session and had to stop just when you were starting to open up." Dr. Riggio looked at Constance. "Shall we pick up where we left off?"

Constance shrugged. "I guess so. Can't keep running from the elephant in the room."

"No, we can't."

"Well, Doc, it's your show. Serve up the questions, and I'll try to answer 'em."

Dr. Riggio started the timer on her desk and then studied Constance for what seemed like an hour. Her gaze was so intense that it made the typically confident woman fidget nervously in her seat.

"You admitted at the end of our last session that you are a lesbian. Let's start there. When did you know you like women?"

Constance took a deep breath and then exhaled. She stared up at the ceiling while searching the annals of her mind.

"I kissed a girl for the first time when I was nine years old at our church youth Summer Christian camp. The girl whom I kissed was named Shelly. She was a Creole girl from New Orleans. She'd come to Chicago to spend the Summer with her grandmother, Sister Florence, a longstanding church member.

"Summer camp used to be held at this park out in Deerfield. It had a lot of trees—it looked more like a forest. All the boys liked Shelly— perfect brown cocoa colored skin. Long silky hair. She even had curves at that age. Anyway, we ditched one of the bible study sessions and snuck off into the woods. We talked for a while, and then we started holding hands. The next thing I knew, we were face-to-face…and then kissed."

"Unbeknownst to us, the woman teaching the bible study session sent this boy named Jeffrey out to find us. Jeffrey was around ten, and he had the biggest crush on Shelly. He found us in the woods right when we kissed. All I heard was, 'Oooo…I'm tellin'!" Constance smirked while she stared at the floor and recounted what happened. "Jeffrey started running back toward those tents, and Shelly and I took off after him."

"Did you catch him?"

"Usain Bolt wouldn't have caught that boy. He was mad it wasn't him kissing her."

"What happened?"

"To make a long story short, he told on us, and our parents were informed." Constance stared at the floor again. Frown lines streaked across her forehead. "Shelly's grandmother was so upset that she took her out of camp—I believe she may have sent her back to Louisiana, I'm not sure. What I do know is that I never saw Shelly again. And I never saw her grandmother again. Sister Florence stopped coming to our church."

Dr. Riggio scribbled in her notepad.

"So, that was your first kiss?"

Constance shook her head. "I didn't say that was my first kiss. I said that was the first time I kissed a girl. Although we were busted and things got crazy afterward, I enjoyed the experience—I wanted it. Now, the first time I was kissed…that's a different story."

"Care to share?" Dr. Riggio asked.

Constance rubbed the palms of her clammy hands on her jeans and swallowed hard.

"It happened a few months before my encounter with Shelly. It was at the church."

She gripped the ring on her right index finger and turned it counterclockwise. Her leg trembled, and her upper torso swayed slightly. It was as if the truth sloshed and swirled inside her, surging through her limbs as it slowly made its way upward to spill from her mouth eventually.

Dr. Riggio was experienced enough to know when a patient was on the verge of opening up. She didn't dare interrupt or offer Constance an easy way out. The best strategy was to remain quiet while Constance assembled her words...her thoughts—and Dr. Riggio allowed that space for her words and her thoughts to connect.

"We were at bible study one night. After it was over, my dad was in his office counseling one of the members. I had to clean up the church with Deacon Jones—my dad's right-hand man. Everyone else had gone home." Constance paused to clear her throat. "So, I umm...I was sweeping, and Deacon Jones grabbed me from behind. He pulled me to him and made me sit on his lap. His breath was hot. He kissed my ear. I could feel his...you know what I'm saying."

Dr. Riggio nodded.

"He whispered something in my ear. I couldn't tell you what he said because I was so nervous that all I could hear was the thump from my heart. He gripped my chin and forced me to look at him. He kissed me on the lips. It was just a peck, but it still made me want to vomit." Constance dabbed at a tear, threatening to break free from the corner of her eye. "I know now that what he was doing is called sexual abuse, which is inappropriate touching without my consent. Also, looking back, I guess he was always grooming me...he gave me gifts, checked on me when my dad was away on church business, and other things. Each touch after that became more intimate."

"How long did it go on?"

"Until I was a teenager." The tear she'd vanquished seconds earlier returned and broke free. "I admit, as I got older, I became disgusted by the way he placed his hand in the center of my lower back and sneakily slid his hand across my butt after he released me from a hug."

"Did you ever tell anyone?"

"I couldn't. He was my dad's best friend and, after my dad, the most respected person in the church. I kept it to myself until I couldn't."

Dr. Riggio handed Constance the tissue box. Constance snatched a few pieces of tissue and dabbed her eyes.

"What do you mean?"

Constance sighed. "When I was sixteen, he…he molested me. I'm not sure why then, but he did. It happened in the basement of the church. There used to be a bed down there. It was after bible study again. My dad was traveling. Deacon Jones told my mom he'd bring me home. I lost my virginity to a monster…and gained a child." Constance began to sob uncontrollably. Dr. Riggio sat quietly and waited until she regained her composure.

"So, he impregnated you?"

Constance nodded.

"Is that when your parents found out?"

"Yes, they found out I was pregnant, but they didn't find out Deacon Jones was the father."

"Who did they think was the father?"

"You remember that boy, Jeffrey, I told you about—the one who caught Shelly and me in the woods kissing?"

"Yes."

"I knew I was pregnant when my monthly cycle was late. I needed someone to blame. Jeffrey begged me to go out with him throughout junior high school, but I wouldn't give him the time of day. All that changed when I found out I was pregnant. I was so desperate for a flunky that I gave Jeffrey much more than the time of day. To this day, he thinks he was my first."

"So, you told your parents that Jeffrey was the father?"

"Yes."

"What happened?"

"Mama was disappointed. Daddy was pissed. He kept screaming, 'You're the pastor's daughter! How could you do something so stupid!'" Constance dabbed at the corners of her eyes again. "I was two months pregnant when I told them. It was on a Saturday. Two days later, my mother drove me to Milwaukee to have an abortion. Two years later, she had to drive me to Milwaukee again. I didn't want to have sex with the Deacon, but he didn't give me much of a choice…I wanted him to stop. He was six-four and two hundred fifty pounds, and I wasn't."

"That time, I blamed a guy named Malik."

"Did Malik agree with the abortion? Did his family know?"

"Malik was in on it. He was a member of our church, and we went to school together. One day, I stayed after school for tutoring. I tried to use the girl's bathroom, but the door was locked. I had to go bad, so I went to the boy's' bathroom. It was more than an hour after school let out, so I figured everyone was gone."

"When I walked into the boy's bathroom, and let's just say…I caught Malik in a compromising position with the school's star quarterback. Malik begged me not to tell. I agreed, under one condition…"

"He agreed to say he was the boy who got you pregnant."

Constance nodded. "Win-win situation."

"After the second abortion, I changed."

"How?"

"I couldn't stand to be touched or even flirted with by a boy. It made my skin crawl. That's when I started keeping company with girls."

"You dated girls openly?"

"Nooo…and embarrass my dad? I don't think so. I was going to take my desire to be with girls to my grave. But that plan went left when my mom barged into my bedroom without knocking and caught me and my "study partner," Kim, bumping and grinding on my bed."

"What was the fallout from that?"

"I wasn't allowed to hang out with Kim anymore. After high school, I was forced to choose a college out of state—they felt I needed to get out of Chicago." Constance smirked. "Sending me away for college just gave me more freedom to explore. When I returned home from college, I had cut my long hair, was rocking a fade, and didn't own one dress."

"How did your parents react?"

"My dad gave me an ultimatum. I could date and marry Clarence—my ex-husband—or be banished from the family and cut out of his will."

"Did your husband ever learn that your father forced you to marry him?"

"Well, Clarence signed the Non-Disclosure Agreement my dad put in front of him. He also accepted the monthly $5,000 payments that my dad deposited into his bank account through Deacon Jones' company… my parents couldn't risk getting audited and the world finding out that the world-renowned Bishop Ed Harrington was paying to hide the fact that his only daughter was a lesbian."

"So, your mother knew?"

"No, I don't think she knew, it was done through my dad."

Dr. Riggio took a deep breath and exhaled. She closed her notebook, looked at Constance, and said, "That's a lot to unpack."

"Well, you wanted my truth…you got it."

"I appreciate you trusting me enough to tell me your story. How do you feel now that you've shared it?"

Constance wiggled her shoulders. "It's weird. I feel looser."

"I'm not surprised. It helps when we can share our internal secrets out loud. I hope you will begin your healing journey; you've been carrying a lot of emotional baggage for many years."

"Yes, I have." Constance adjusted her posture and stared directly into Dr. Riggio's eyes. "I have a confession."

"This is the perfect place to confess." Dr. Riggio glanced at her wristwatch. "And we still have a few minutes left in our session. Go ahead."

"For years, I have asked myself a question I can't answer."

"What's the question?"

Constance fiddled with her ring again. She inhaled, exhaled, and then said, "I've wondered whether I was born liking women...a lesbian *or* did my experience with Deacon Jones sway my decision to like girls... women...and become a lesbian? I know that I had interest in girls before the molestation, but I was young and did not connect living a life as a lesbian versus acting on my thoughtless childhood desires."

The patient and the doctor stared at each other. Constance's questions hovered between them like the morning fog over the San Francisco Bay. Dr. Riggio could see the confusion on Constance's face. Constance could see the apprehension on Dr. Riggio's face. The question was complex and, arguably, the most divisive question in Christianity today. These questions had caused many controversial conversations in churches across the country, and now it had been uttered in their safe place.

Dr. Riggio's lips parted slowly after pondering on each question. Just as her responses were about to spill from her mouth, the timer buzzed.

"Out of time," Constance said.

"For now," Dr. Riggio replied.

CHAPTER 7

Katherine swiftly sat upright in bed, her heart racing as she struggled to shake off the remnants of the vivid dream that had invaded her sleep. The moonlight filtered through her bedroom window, casting shadows that danced eerily across the walls.

She was twelve again in her dream, wandering through the church's familiar halls, the air thick with the scent of old wood and musty hymnals. She felt drawn to the basement, a place she'd always been warned to avoid. Curiosity propelled her forward, each step echoing in the silence.

The basement door creaked open, revealing a dimly lit room cluttered with forgotten relics of faith. The atmosphere was stifling, heavy with an unsettling energy. As she descended the steps, a chill crept up her spine. In the dream, she turned to find a figure lurking in the shadows—someone she thought she could trust.

The scene twisted, warping into something sinister. A chilling silence replaced the laughter that had once filled those walls, and Katherine felt the weight of fear settle in her chest. She wanted to run, but her feet felt glued to the floor, her body motionless, and her scream loud and silent simultaneously.

Suddenly, the warmth of her childhood faith turned cold, suffocating her as memories collided with the nightmares. The details faded, leaving her breathless and shaken. The room around her felt too small, too confining, as the shadows stretched longer, enveloping her.

Katherine gasped, her eyes darting around the familiar room, reality crashing back in waves. She pulled the covers tighter around her, feeling both the weight of her dreams and the burden of her past. The church, once a sanctuary, now loomed in her mind, a complex tapestry of light and dark.

Sitting there in the stillness of the night, she felt a deep ache for the girl she once was, a longing for safety and understanding. She reached for her bedside lamp with trembling hands, illuminating the room with a warm glow as if to push back the darkness lingering in her thoughts.

Pastor Doug jolted awake as the bedside lamp flickered to life, flooding the room with soft light. Blinking away sleep, he turned to find Katherine sitting up, her face pale and drawn. Concern washed over him instantly.

"Kat? What's wrong?" he asked, his voice thick with worry.

She looked at him, her eyes shimmering with unshed tears.

"Nothing!"

Katherine shook her head and tried lying back down, but Doug gently grabbed her forearm.

"Babe, you can talk to me."

"Not about this," Katherine said, pools of water forming in her eyes.

Doug sat up until his back touched the headboard. He draped his arm around Katherine's trembling shoulders and pulled her close. "Babe, you can talk to me about anything. I'm your husband. I'm here to support you, not judge you."

The tear that twinkled in the corner of Katherine's eye spilled and streaked down her right cheek and Doug's left cheek where her face rested.

"I had a nightmare… about the basement," she confessed, her voice barely a whisper.

Doug's brow furrowed, confusion mixing with a protective instinct. "The basement? What basement?"

"The church's basement."

"What happened?"

Taking a shaky breath, Katherine's hands trembled. "It felt so real, Doug. I was twelve… and your father…" She hesitated, the weight of the words pressing heavily on her. "He—he hurt me."

The air felt thick and electric as the realization dawned on him. A wave of shock washed over his face, and for a moment, he was at a loss for words. His mind raced, struggling to reconcile the image of his father with the pain Katherine was recounting.

"It was just a dream, baby," Doug whispered, pulling her closer.

"No! It's not just a dream."

"What do you mean?"

"Doug, it really happened! Your dad, really…"

Katherine's words trailed off as if a stiff breeze had swept them away.

Confusion dominated Doug's face. That confusion made its way to his tone. "My dad?" he finally managed, disbelief creeping into his tone. "Katherine, are you sure?"

She nodded, tears spilling down her cheeks. "I never told you. I thought I could bury it, forget, but it keeps haunting me."

Doug's heart sank, the gravity of her revelation settling like lead in his chest. He took her hand into his, feeling the tremor of her fingers. "I had no idea. I'm so sorry," he murmured, the pain in his chest mingling with a fierce protectiveness. "You shouldn't have gone through that alone."

The vulnerability between them deepened as she looked into his eyes, searching for solace. In that moment, he understood the layers of her suffering—and the complexities that lay ahead.

"Do you want to talk about it?"

Katherine shook her head. "No."

"Babe, this is weighing on you. You need to talk about it."

Katherine sobbed. "I can't—not with you."

"Shh, don't cry." Doug kissed her forehead. "I understand you are uncomfortable talking to me, but I know who you can talk to. My therapist, Dr. Riggio."

Katherine sat in Dr. Riggio's office, the familiar tension in her shoulders easing slightly in the comforting environment. Sunlight streamed through the window, illuminating the room's warm tones—a contrast to the darkness that had haunted her nights. She glanced at the bookshelf filled with various titles on psychology and self-help, a subtle reminder that she was in a space dedicated to healing.

Dr. Riggio leaned slightly forward in her chair. "Your husband mentioned you were having nightmares when I spoke to him on the phone. He said you had some things that you needed to talk about. Do you want to tell me how you're feeling? More specifically, let's talk about your nightmares."

Katherine took a deep breath, the air thick with the weight of her memories. "They feel so real," she began, her voice trembling. "In my dreams, I'm back in the church basement. It's dark, and I can't escape.

I can hear echoes of laughter that turn into whispers... then into something sinister."

As she spoke, her gaze drifted to the window, her mind conjuring the imagery of her dreams.

"I see shadows moving, and I know something terrible will happen. It's like, I'm that twelve-year-old girl again, trapped, powerless, and voiceless."

Dr. Riggio nodded, her expression focused and empathetic. "That sounds incredibly frightening. How do you feel when you wake up from those dreams?"

Katherine's brow furrowed as she recalled the feelings that followed. "I'm drenched in sweat, and my heart feels like it's going to burst. It's as if I'm carrying that fear with me every day. I can't shake it off."

She paused for a moment, considering her words. "It's understandable that such vivid memories would resurface in your dreams, especially when you're processing your trauma. Do you think a specific event or emotion triggers these nightmares?"

"I'm unsure...I never thought about that or what happens before the nightmares."

"We all have triggers. When we are awake, we have the ability to tuck what's bothering us away so that we can continue living life. But when we go to sleep, sometimes that Pandora's box that we lock our thoughts away in opens, and those thoughts we tucked away during the day come to life. Those suppressed thoughts transform into our subconscious mind, forming our dreams."

Katherine nodded in agreement. It was as if the doctor's words had solved a riddle that stuck her between two worlds. She couldn't understand why, after years of being able to suppress her troubled childhood, her past was now taunting her both mentally and emotionally.

"I've been having these bad dreams about my childhood for the past six or seven months."

"What life-altering changes have occurred in your life during that time?" Dr. Riggio asked.

"Well, my husband has taken over his father's church."

"So, you're now the "First Lady" of the church?"

"Yes."

"That's got to be a little intimidating. I've never been to your husband's church, but I understand it's big."

"Over six thousand members," Katherine tossed out.

"Wow."

"That's a lot of eyes on you."

Katherine nodded.

"How does that make you feel?"

"Vulnerable."

"Watched."

Katherine hesitated, the memories swirling in her mind. "I think…I think being the "First Lady" of the church where I was violated makes me feel exposed. When I'm reminded of my past or feel any hint of fear in my life, it's like the nightmares are a way of reliving that trauma, forcing me to confront it."

"Confrontation can be an important part of healing," Dr. Riggio said while scribbling on her notepad. "But it can also be painful. What do you wish your dreams would tell you if you could choose?"

Katherine closed her eyes for a moment, envisioning a different scenario. "I wish they could show me strength instead of fear. I want to feel empowered, to confront the darkness instead of being consumed by it."

"That's a powerful intention, Katherine. Exploring ways to reclaim that sense of strength while awake might be helpful. Visualization techniques, perhaps, or grounding exercises when you wake from the nightmares."

Katherine nodded slowly, feeling a flicker of hope ignite within her. "I'd like that. I want to change the narrative."

Dr. Riggio leaned back, contemplating her response.

"I'm curious…what did Doug say when you told him about the abuse at the hands of his father?"

"He was supportive. He apologized for his dad's actions."

"That's good. You're going to need your husband's ongoing support even through it has been two years since the revelation of you telling him about the abuse."

Suddenly, Katherine's eyes drifted toward the floor-to-ceiling window in the right corner of the office. Cars raced past on the busy highway outside. Dr. Riggio followed Katherine's gaze.

"Katherine…are you okay?"

Katherine nodded. "Yes," she mumbled. "Your question has made me think."

"About what?"

Katherine's head turned robotically, and she stared at Dr. Riggio.

"If I told you that your dad was a molester, would you believe me?"

"I'd have a hard time believing that my dad could hurt a child…a young girl."

"Doug didn't even push back. He didn't even challenge me when I told him that his father molested me when I was a little girl."

Katherine's head turned robotically again, and her eyes fixed on the window. "His reaction has me wondering…" she paused for a minute and then murmured, "…did he already know?"

CHAPTER 8

Clarence drove a 2015 BMW 650i Grand Coupe. The sticker price in 2015 was $86,000. When Clarence made it clear to Bishop Ed Harrington that he wanted the car in 2020, the cost was $42,000. The look on the faces of his co-workers when he pulled into the parking lot of the company where he worked at the time was priceless.

With the Midwest sun spraying the usually windy city with bright rays that forced commuters to wear sunglasses, Clarence pulled his dream car into a gas station to give it something to drink. While filling the gas tank, he learned a valuable lesson—pay close attention to the energy you put out because it would become the energy you attract.

"Nice ride, bruh!"

Looking down at his cell phone while fueling his 8-cylinder beast, Clarence was startled and swiftly gazed upward. A tall, husky man stood staring from the other side of the gas pump while filling up a white panel van.

"Thanks!" Clarence said, looking at his phone again.

"How many cylinders?" the man asked.

"Eight," Clarence replied without looking up.

He could feel more questions looming, so he abruptly ended the fueling session roughly five gallons before his car's tank was filled.

It was his turn to cook for him and Malcolm. He craved a shoulder blade steak, garlic potatoes, and steamed cauliflower, so he headed into the supermarket next door to the gas station.

Clarence spent fifteen minutes in the supermarket perusing the aisles. When he returned to his car, his stomach was breakdancing with hunger pains, he quickly turned the ignition. The engine roared when he started the vehicle, but Clarence didn't immediately pull out of the parking space. Why? Because the man sitting in the back seat of his car asked him a question that required an answer.

"You wanna die today?"

Clarence shook his head violently.

The man in his backseat pressed the barrel of his gun against Clarence's occipital bone.

"I didn't hear you answer. So, I'm gon' ask you again…do you wanna die today?"

"No," Clarence managed to answer through trembling lips.

"Good. Well, if you don't want this to be your last day on earth, you'll do exactly as I say."

Clarence nodded but quickly remembered the attacker from the gas station in his backseat. Realizing he didn't respond to nonverbal replies, he promptly uttered, "Okay."

Clarence drove to a nearby park. He followed a winding road that led to the rear of the park, where the groundskeeper's shed was located. The area looked like it hadn't been cut since the Jurassic era. If not for the dirt road, he could have easily veered off into the deep, dark woods, and his car would have been hidden for months.

As he pulled up to the spot where the gunman had told him to park, Clarence immediately noticed a familiar face. Standing next to a white van parked a few yards away was the man who'd asked him questions about his car while he pumped gas.

"Get out," the gunman ordered. "And if you try to run, it'll be the last time you run anywhere."

Clarence hurriedly stepped out of his car, the door screeching softly behind him. He paused for a moment, taking in the dense thicket ahead, where tangled underbrush and towering shrubs created a wild, untamed atmosphere.

"Okay…walk toward the van over there," the gunman said.

As Clarence moved forward, he picked his way carefully through the lush greenery, the earthy scent of damp soil and moss mingling in the air. Sunlight filtered through the leaves above, casting dappled shadows on the ground as he navigated the winding path, his footsteps muffled by the thick carpet of fallen leaves and grass.

With the gun pressed in the center of his back, Clarence stumbled toward the burly man. He immediately noticed the size of the guy's hand, the scar on his forehead, and the deadly look in his eyes. He didn't have to hear rumors or wonder about the man's capability. Clarence was street-smart enough to recognize that the man known as Gutter was a natural-born killer.

"You Clarence, right?"

"Yes."

"Good. I'm glad to know we got the right dude."

"Who are you?"

"That's not important," Gutter said and stepped forward. "Here's what you need to know…I can touch you anytime I want. Do you understand me?"

"Yes."

"You're one of those IT nerds, right?"

Clarence nodded.

"That means you're pretty smart, right?"

Clarence nodded again.

"I figured you are. So, you've probably figured out why my buddy with the Glock aimed at your head snatched you up and brought you here."

"Yes."

"Let me hear you say why you think you're here."

Clarence's voice trembled, and tears streamed down his cheek. When he felt the gun barrel press against the back of his head, the crotch of his pants suddenly became soaked.

"I'm here because of what I told Pastor Doug."

"You are smart," Gutter said and pointed at Clarence. He took another step closer. "Now, you're going to do something for me to ensure you will no longer threaten my friend—Pastor Doug—again."

Gutter grabbed Clarence's right ear and twisted. The pain brought Clarence to his knees.

"Get up!" Gutter barked.

Clarence struggled to his feet, sobbing like a child with a toothache.

"I don't trust you," Gutter growled. "You know why?"

"No," Clarence muttered.

"I don't trust you because you're trying to blackmail Pastor Doug is a good dude. And I understand he's never done anything wrong to you. But, you chose to come after him. Any man who would do something that lowdown isn't worth being trusted. You get me?"

"Yes," Clarence muttered. "I'm sorry."

"Bruh, your actions speak so loud that I can't hear what you're saying. So, I have a plan. You're going to do something that will ensure you ain't gon' mess with my friend again. And if you don't do what I expect of you, I will prove how badly I can hurt you...*and* the people you care about."

Gutter tightened his grip on Clarence's ear and led him to the rear of the van. Gutter opened the van's back door. Inside the van, Malcolm was tied up with a gag in his mouth.

Clarence looked as if he'd seen a ghost. His eyes widened, and more tears spilled.

"Clarence, if you don't cooperate," Gutter said, "I'm gon' first deal with your boyfriend," Gutter slammed the back door of the van shut, "and then I'm gon' deal with you."

"Do you understand me?"

"**Yes!**" Clarence screamed.

The gunman chuckled and said, "Bruh, you might wanna let go of this boy's ear."

"Why?"

"Because first, you made him pee in his pants." The man used his free hand to pinch his nostrils. "Now, he's doing number two." They both laughed out loud.

CHAPTER 9

If Pareto's Principle was true—eighty percent of outcomes resulted from twenty percent of causes—then eighty percent of the wealth generated by churches in America was generated by only twenty percent of the country's churches. And since Shekinah Holy Temple, with its congregation of nearly seven thousand members and pending second church location, was one of the largest black churches in the city, it's safe to say that Shekinah was a member of that twenty percent club; thus, making it no surprise that as the leader of Shekinah Holy Temple, Pastor Douglas Harrington III lifestyle would reflect his church's prosperity.

One week after taking over the position immediately vacated by his father, Pastor Doug's family was extracted from their humble abode and relocated to a nearly 10,000-square-foot mini-mansion in Woodland Park—an exclusive community in Deerfield, Illinois, a suburb of Chicago—where tree-lined streets and meticulously landscaped yards created a sense of serene suburban luxury.

The community was within walking distance of several prominent landmarks. To the north, the Deerfield Historic Village was a short drive away, offering a glimpse into the town's rich history with its collection of 19th-century homes and buildings. To the east, you could find Deerbrook Mall, with its upscale shops, restaurants, and cafes, providing a blend of convenience and leisure. A bit further, the Chicago Botanic Garden was a favorite destination for nature lovers, offering sprawling gardens and walking trails that were especially beautiful in spring and summer.

The gated neighborhood where Pastor Doug and his family resided also featured a private park with playgrounds, tennis courts, and walking paths, all manicured and polished to perfection. Despite its proximity to these amenities, the house and its community felt secluded, offering both the benefits of suburban life and the privacy and exclusivity of gated living.

Their house was a two-story brick and stone residence, blending modern and traditional architecture. A green picturesque golf course lawn spread across the front yard, bordered by beds of vibrant flowers and tall, graceful maple trees that offered shade and privacy. A stone pathway led to the front door, a grand entryway framed by elegant pillars and arched windows.

The home's exterior was rich with detail—exposed wooden beams along the roofline, slate shingles, and soft, warm lighting that highlighted its beauty during the evening hours. Large windows, trimmed in white, allowed plenty of natural light to spill into the open floor plan inside.

To the right of the house, a winding driveway snaked toward a five-car garage. A stone patio with a built-in grill and seating area in the backyard provided a perfect spot for outdoor entertaining and meditation. The meticulously maintained backyard lawn stretched toward a line of tall trees, which separated the property from the golf course of Deerfield Golf Club. Although the thick foliage kept the home private and peaceful, the cursing and venting of a golfer looking for a ball he'd shanked into the woods could sometimes be heard in the distance.

Inside, the home featured spacious rooms, high ceilings, and large windows that brought the beauty of the surrounding nature indoors. Pastor Doug could be found every morning as the sun ascended, sitting at the large kitchen table sipping his steaming black coffee.

His fingers curled around a coffee cup handle on this cold, and windy Saturday morning in December. The kitchen was bathed in soft morning light, the sun casting long shadows across the polished granite countertops and stainless-steel appliances. The room was quiet, except for the faint ticking of the wall clock and the occasional sound of Doug tapping his fingers absently against the side of his cup. His brow was furrowed, his gaze distant, locked in the dark whirl of his thoughts.

He barely registered the sound of footsteps behind him until Katherine appeared in the doorway. She wore a thick red robe, and her hair was pulled back into a neat ponytail. She was as quiet as a mouse, but the concern etched on her face was unmistakable.

"Hey, honey," Doug said when he noticed her. "How long have you been standing there?"

"Long enough to know you're upset."

"Babe, I'm not upset."

"Doug, this is me you're talking to, not one of your church members who only sees you on Sundays. I've been married to you long enough to know when something has you worried," Katherine said in a soft voice. "What's going on?"

Doug glanced at her, his eyes heavy with a weight she couldn't quite place. He sighed and set the coffee mug down, wrapping both hands around it as though grounding himself to the moment.

"I'm going to see my mother today," he said with a low and measured voice.

Katherine's face softened. "It's been a while, hasn't it?"

Doug nodded, his gaze drifting back to the dark liquid in his mug. "Yeah…too long," he murmured. "She sits in that house, all alone. I know I haven't had time to visit, and I doubt William or Constance have. I don't know if she even sees anyone besides the housekeeper."

Katherine sat across from him and reached for his hand. "Do you want me to come with you?"

Doug shook his head slowly, his expression turning resolute. "No," he said firmly, though his tone was still gentle. "I need to go alone. We have a lot of issues to unpack between us, and I must handle it on my terms."

She hesitated, her thumb brushing over the back of his hand. "Are you sure? I know how difficult this is for you."

"I'm sure." He looked up at her then, his gaze steady.

"Can you tell me what you plan on discussing with her?"

Doug sipped his coffee and nodded. "I plan on asking her to go see Dr. Riggio."

Katherine rocked back in her seat, crossed her arms, and shook her head. "Good luck with that. No disrespect, but your mom is one of the most stubborn and insolent people I know, Doug. I can't see her opening up about family business to a psychiatrist. She is from the old school of life; they were taught to keep their secrets under the rug, buried in dust."

"I know," he interrupted softly, not wanting to start a debate, "but we can't keep putting this off. I can tell she's been struggling, and Dr. Riggio might be able to help Mom figure out how to sort through some things. I don't believe we, as a family, will ever be able to move on from the trauma and dark secrets of our past unless *everyone* deals with their version and truth of their past, including her."

Katherine's mouth opened as though to protest, but she stopped herself, biting back her words. She could see the concern and desperation in his eyes.

Instead, she placed her hand on top of his hand and said, "I support you."

Pastor Doug approached the sprawling, 12,600-square-foot house nestled deep within the gated community. It was the property that his parents once shared. Now, its only occupant was Eleanor Harrington, the matriarch of the Harrington family.

The property sat at the end of a winding, cobblestone driveway flanked by tall, well-manicured hedges that offered privacy and a sense of regal isolation. The house was a grand blend of modern architecture and traditional charm, its exterior clad in pale stone and weathered brick, softened by climbing ivy vines.

An expansive front porch wrapped around the house, supported by thick white columns that added a stately air to the otherwise quiet and reclusive residence. The front door, crafted from dark mahogany with intricate carvings, bore an elegance reminiscent of old-world estates. Above the door, a large, arched window allowed the afternoon sunlight to spill into the entrance hall.

The lawn was immaculate, dotted with perfectly pruned bushes, flower beds bursting with deep reds and purples, and a small koi pond off to the side, complete with a trickling waterfall that added a constant whisper of movement to the otherwise still scene.

Inside, the home was no less impressive. High ceilings and wide hallways gave the place an airy, almost echoing quality. The foyer led into a grand living room where floor-to-ceiling windows provided a stunning view of the landscaped backyard, framed by heavy velvet drapes. Eleanor spent most of her time there—surrounded by antique furniture, family heirlooms, and relics from her time as the First Lady of the Church.

The décor was understated but elegant—soft cream walls, dark wood accents, and the occasional burst of color from a well-placed painting or vase. The house felt as though it was frozen in time, a shrine to her past, untouched by the world outside. The quiet stillness inside mirrored Eleanor's reclusive existence, where each room, though perfectly kept, bore the weight of long, unspoken memories.

Despite its size and grandeur, the house had a peaceful, lonely atmosphere. As Doug walked through its vast halls, he could feel the distance that had grown between them, not just physically but emotionally. Each room echoed the absence of warmth and connection that once was. As he approached his mother's home office, where she could usually be found, he paused outside the door, took a deep breath, and exhaled before entering.

The late afternoon sun streamed through the large windows, casting a warm golden light across the office. The walls were lined with portraits of past events: a photo of her on the golf course with Hillary Clinton, a photo of her standing next to Oprah Winfrey, a photo of her and her late husband standing in front of the Eiffel Tower, and other impressive photographs with nationally known church leaders.

The sun glistened over her as she sat at her mahogany desk, fingers trembling over the papers scattered before her. Each document was a reminder of a not-too-distant past—old memorandums, speeches, and other remnants of her former role at the church.

Eleanor was startled when she heard the knock at her office door. "Who is it?"

The door opened slightly, and Doug peered inside. "It's me, Mama."

"Dougie!" Eleanor stood and moved around to the front of her desk as fast as her arthritis would allow. "It's so good to see you."

They embraced, and Doug could feel his mother's sincerity. She was obviously lonely, and knowing that his failure to visit more contributed to her current state, caused an ocean of sadness to sweep over him.

"What are you doing, Mama?"

"Nothing. Just sitting in here trying to clean up."

Doug scanned the office. To his surprise, it was more cluttered than he could remember ever seeing it. His mother was a neat freak, so it was shocking to see a desk covered with papers, dust bunnies on the bookshelf, a coffee mug with lipstick stains on the rim, and the residue of spilled coffee at its base.

They sat in the two high-back guest chairs in front of her desk.

"Mama, are you okay?"

"I'm fine, baby. Like I said—"

"Mama," he grabbed her hand, "this is me you're talking to. You know, we have always kept it real with each other. Back in the day, I knew that there was one person on the planet I could share my secrets with, and they wouldn't go anywhere, and that person was you."

"I know, baby," Eleanor said and nodded.

"Remember that time my friends and I robbed that liquor store, and I ran inside the house huffing and puffing, out of breath?"

"I remember," Eleanor said and smiled.

"You came into my room and saw me shoving the gun under my mattress. When I turned around and saw you staring at me on my knees, trying to shove the gun into the middle of my mattress, you looked at me and said something. Do you remember what you said?"

"Take that thing out of my house. A better place to hide it would be inside the hollow part of that old oak tree in the backyard." The corners of her mouth curled upward. "The police still found the gun, so I don't know how good my suggestion was." She chuckled.

"Yeah, but it wasn't because it was a bad hiding spot. Actually, it was a brilliant hiding spot. The police found the gun because I messed up and told Jo-Jo and Gutter where I hid the gun. When the police caught Jo-Jo, he ratted on me and Gutter and told the police where I hid it."

Eleanor stared aimlessly at the floor for a bit and then looked into her son's eyes.

"Dougie, no one knows you better than I do. Something is on your mind. What's the real reason you came here?"

Doug tried to avoid eye contact with his mother, but she gripped his chin and forced him to look at her. After taking another deep breath, he said what he came there to say.

"Mama, this family has a lot of secrets... secrets that have crippled us in many ways. Everyone in the family goes to counseling to try to heal and move forward, but this family can't truly move on until the family matriarch confronts the root of our family's dark past, too."

"I know how private you are." He looked around the office. "But I can also see your depression. Mama, you would've never allowed this office to get this untidy when Dad was alive." He looked back at Eleanor and saw a tear streak down her cheek. He used his thumb to swipe it away. "I would like to think I haven't asked you for much."

"You haven't," Eleanor whispered.

"Well, I'm asking you for something now. Please consider seeing Dr. Riggio." His voice was barely above a whisper. "For us, Mom."

The silence hung between them for a long moment, thick with unspoken fears and the heavy air of unresolved tension. Eleanor finally nodded, though it was reluctant, her gaze falling to the floor.

"Okay," she whispered. "I'll go, I'm ready."

Doug exhaled slowly, nodding as he squeezed her hand. "Thank you," he said softly, though the gratitude in his voice carried an undercurrent of something darker—an unspoken worry that her session with Dr. Riggio might unveil things that could do more damage than good.

He believed that God would begin to heal his family through his mother's confession of her past and their dad's family secrets.

As he walked away, he couldn't help but wonder, *Will she open up to Dr. Riggio?*

CHAPTER 10

Eleanor glanced at the clock: 3:55 PM. In five minutes, she would meet with Dr. Riggio. Her heart raced, and she thought about the facade she had carefully constructed over the years. To the world, she was the perfect First Lady—graceful, poised, and unwavering. But inside, she felt like a dam was about to burst, holding back secrets that threatened to spill into the open like a gushing wave.

She smoothed her blouse and ran her fingers through her perfectly bob-cut, salt-and-pepper hair, attempting to dispel the unease that coiled within her. She knew the importance of this meeting, but the thought of exposing her life and vulnerabilities to a stranger filled her with dread.

What if she revealed too much?

What if her secrets were not just hers to bear?

Taking a deep breath, she walked to the door with an insecure confidence, pausing momentarily. Inhaling sharply, she stepped into the office corridor, her heels echoing softly against the marble floors. As she approached the waiting area, the soft murmur of voices and paper rustling faded into the background.

"How may I help you, ma'am?" the receptionist asked.

Eleanor leaned in to avoid being heard by the two women in the lobby and whispered, "My name is Eleanor Harrington. I'm here to see Dr. Riggio."

Understanding the silver fox's desire for privacy, the receptionist leaned forward and said, "She's been expecting you." She gestured toward the hallway. "Go through that door and go to the end of the hallway. You'll see a door marked "Dr. Riggio" on the left."

Eleanor mouthed, "Thank You," and went through the door. Her mind raced as she walked down the long hallway toward Dr. Riggio's office, questioning her decision to see a therapist.

Would Dr. Riggio understand?

Could she be trusted with secrets?

With a final, deep breath, she placed a smile on her face, turned the knob, and stepped inside. The office was warm and inviting, adorned with soothing colors and artwork that whispered reassurance. Dr. Riggio's kind eyes met Eleanor; oddly, she felt a sense of safety, allowing her to form an instant bond.

"Mrs. Harrington," she said, extending a hand. "It's a pleasure to meet you."

"Thank you," Eleanor replied, her voice steadier than she felt.

As Eleanor took a seat across from Dr. Riggio, she caught a glimpse of herself in a small mirror on the wall—her poised exterior contrasting sharply with the turmoil within.

The large carved wood-trimmed and paneless windows let in the afternoon light, and the faint scent of lavender filled the room. Yet, Eleanor couldn't relax. She never wanted to be here and hadn't even considered therapy until Doug's plea a few days earlier. But something had shifted inside her, some quiet realization that the past wouldn't stay buried forever.

"Shall we begin?"

Dr. Riggio asked gently, settling into her chair.

Eleanor sat stiffly in the leather chair across from Dr. Riggio, her hands folded neatly in her lap, eyes cast downward as though avoiding the weight on her shoulders. Her heart rapidly raced, but she knew she had taken the first step. She was ready to confront the secrets in her past and the shadows that had followed her for too long.

Dr. Riggio, a calm presence with sharp, perceptive eyes behind wire-rimmed glasses, sat across from her in a posture of quiet patience. She asked Eleanor a few introductory questions—about her health, her family, the usual pleasantries—but they both knew that wasn't why Eleanor had come. They were circling something darker, something buried deep beneath the polished surface of her carefully maintained composure.

After a moment of silence, Dr. Riggio leaned forward slightly, her voice gentle but probing. "Eleanor, can we talk about your husband?"

Eleanor's body tensed at the mention of Ed. She hadn't said his name in months, not in any meaningful way. *Bishop.* That's what people had called him, a title spoken with reverence that no longer felt justified.

"Ed," Eleanor said softly, her voice barely above a whisper. "He's been gone for about a year."

"I know," Dr. Riggio replied, observing her. "But I imagine his presence still lingers, doesn't it? Especially given his role in the church… and in your life."

Eleanor swallowed, her throat suddenly dry. She nodded, unable to find the words yet knowing exactly where this was going. She could *feel* it—the questions she had spent years avoiding were about to be asked.

"From everything I've read," Dr. Riggio continued, her tone still soft but unwavering, "he was a *very* powerful man of God. Respected. Charismatic. But...there were whispers, weren't there?"

Eleanor's heart tightened with an old familiar pang that had never fully gone away. She glanced up, meeting Dr. Riggio's eyes for the first time since she sat down. "There were always whispers," she said, her voice tinged with bitterness she hadn't intended to reveal.

"About him," Dr. Riggio prompted gently, "or about you?"

The question hung in the air, sharp and uncomfortable. Eleanor let out a slow breath, her mind drifting back to the early days, to the sermons, the crowds, the adoration—and to the darker corners of their lives, the things whispered behind closed doors, the secrets no one dared to bring to light.

"Both," she admitted, her voice barely audible. "But mostly about him."

Dr. Riggio waited, sensing the fragile balance of the moment. "You sat beside him, in front of the entire congregation, for years... decades, so to speak. Supported him. But...Eleanor, did you know what was happening?"

The words struck her like a blow. Her lips trembled slightly, and she fought to keep her composure. She knew. She had always known, hadn't she? But knowing was different than *acting*. Knowing was different than *speaking out*.

"There were things," she began, her voice unsteady. "Things I didn't want to believe at first. People came to me—women, mostly. They tried to tell me. They said he was..." She trailed off, unable to finish the sentence. The shame of it all tightened in her chest.

Dr. Riggio didn't rush her. "What did they say, Eleanor?"

Eleanor gripped the arms of the chair now, her knuckles white.

"That he wasn't the man they thought he was. That behind the pulpit, behind the charm, there was something else. Something darker. Control. Abuse. Manipulation. And I...I didn't want to admit it. I told myself it was not true. Not Ed."

Dr. Riggio leaned in slightly, her tone gentle but firm. "But you did see it, didn't you?"

Eleanor's breath caught in her throat. Tears welled in her eyes, but she blinked them away. *She had seen it,* she realized, far more than she had ever admitted, even to herself.

"Yes," she whispered, her voice broken. "I saw it. I saw how he treated them, controlled them, and used them. And I did nothing."

Dr. Riggio nodded slowly, letting the truth settle between them before speaking again. "Why do you think you stayed silent, Eleanor? Why did you let it continue?"

Eleanor's chest felt tight, the guilt suffocating her. She had never asked herself that question—not like this, not in a way that demanded an honest answer.

"I... I was afraid," she confessed, the words tumbling out before she could stop them. "Afraid of him. Afraid of what would happen to the church if people knew. Afraid of what they would think of me. I thought... if I kept quiet, it would all go away. That God would handle it. But He didn't. And neither did I."

Tears finally broke free, rolling down her cheeks. She wiped them away quickly, almost angrily, as if trying to erase the shame she had carried for so long.

"I thought it was my duty to stand by him," she continued, her voice shaking. "I thought I had no choice. But I did, didn't I? I could have stopped him. I should have."

Dr. Riggio's voice was steady, offering her a lifeline through the flood of emotion.

"It's easy to look back and say what should have been done; what could have been don. But you weren't just the wife of an everyday man—he was powerful, he had influence, and you were part of that machine. The guilt you feel, Eleanor, is understandable. But you're here now. You're ready to face it. That's what matters."

Eleanor nodded slowly, though the weight of her past still pressed heavily on her chest. The silence stretched between them once more, but it was different now—filled not with avoidance but with the first cracks of truth breaking through.

For the first time in years, Eleanor felt the full extent of what she had hidden away: the pain, the guilt, and the regret. And though it hurt and nearly broke her, she knew this was only the beginning.

And much to her surprise…she felt like the weight was beginning to move.

Dr. Riggio leaned forward, her eyes warm and steady, framed by soft, graying hair that curled slightly at her temples. She reached out gently, her movements slow and deliberate, and slid Eleanor's glasses off her face. The woman sitting before her barely reacted, her gaze distant, as if tethered to a memory too painful to release.

With quiet compassion, Dr. Riggio pulled a soft cloth from her pocket and wiped the lenses, the motion tender, almost reverent. "Sometimes," she said softly, "it helps to see things more clearly when the weight is lifted—if only for a moment."

Eleanor blinked, her lashes damp, and nodded faintly. Her hands trembled, knotted together as if she could hold herself together through sheer force. Dr. Riggio placed the glasses back on Eleanor's face, adjusting them carefully before sitting back. She offered a gentle smile, giving Eleanor the space to begin.

"My last appointment was canceled. Let's talk about your late husband, Bishop Harrington," Dr. Riggio said, her tone patient and inviting. "Where did it all start, and how did you get here?"

Eleanor inhaled shakily, her chest rising and falling as she gathered the courage to speak. When it came, her voice was low and cracked, like a brittle leaf crushed underfoot. "We didn't have much, typical family. My mama worked, my daddy was in the military, so we moved a lot… he wasn't around much." She paused, her lips pressing together tightly. "I remember the winters most. How cold it was, even inside the house. We had to keep the oven door open to stay warm. Have you ever been so cold your bones ache, Dr. Riggio?"

Dr. Riggio shook her head gently, her expression unwavering. "Yes, I'm listening, Eleanor. Please, go on."

Eleanor nodded, her fingers tightening around each other. "When I was 16, I met Bishop Harrington when he was twenty. My girlfriends and I snuck into a house party. Ed was a sophomore in college. He was a star athlete, the popular boy at school, the larger-than-life figure—his voice could fill a room, you know? Everyone loved him." She paused, a bitter smile tugging her lips. "And then he noticed me."

Dr. Riggio's brow furrowed, but she remained silent, her pen hovering above her notepad.

"I was a shy girl," Eleanor continued, her voice growing softer as if the admission itself made her smaller. "I wasn't the loud type; I was quite shy and did not like to be seen, but when he looked at me, he made me feel like I was…*special*. Like I was somebody worth seeing." Her voice cracked, and she closed her eyes tightly, the memory too vivid, too raw. "It was love at first sight, for me at least; he was so charming, and Lord knows, he could make you feel like you were the only one that ever mattered in the room…the world."

She let out a hollow laugh, shaking her head. "He said I had a spirit that shined brighter than any star, he said God had sent him to guide me. To save me. He did somewhat save me from the good guys," she laughed. "We dated. Married. We have beautiful children and grandchildren. But that came with a significant cost to me, my family, and my life." Her hands trembled, and her gaze dropped to the floor, her shame tangible. "I didn't see it for what it was back then. *I couldn't*. His position and power blinded me, like so many people. Funny as it may be, his influence always overshadowed his dark side—even in his death, Bishop Harrington is still in control! I was just his lovely wife, always in his shadow sitting quietly on the first pew every Sunday morning."

"And what do you see now?" Dr. Riggio asked softly, focusing entirely on Eleanor.

Eleanor swallowed hard, her throat bobbing as she tried to force the words out. "He didn't love me," she whispered, her voice breaking. "Not the way I thought. He groomed me. He saw a girl with nothing and gave her attention, gifts, and promises…I believed him. I married him because I thought it meant something. That *I* meant something. In reality, he needed me to be a picture of perfection. Yes, I played the role well; I learned how to be subservient, the perfect wife, mother, first lady, and anything he needed me to be so that he could become the great Bishop William 'Ed' Harrington."

Tears spilled down her cheeks now, her breaths coming in uneven gasps. "*I knew*! I knew about every secret, every child born and unborn, every affair, every evil deacon, even the girls…" Shame crossed her face as she looked at Dr. Riggio, "…even JoAnn. I knew…know!" Eleanor's loud cry filled Dr. Riggio's office. "There was no excuse. I knew better. And he… he took advantage of my love for him for years. And, I let him. I admit it! I am just as guilty." Eleanor was sobbing uncontrollably. "I could've stopped him…I could've!"

Dr. Riggio leaned in slightly, her voice firm but kind. "Eleanor, his actions were not your fault. You were his victim, too. You were manipulated by someone who had his issues and power over you. You didn't 'let him' do anything. He made his choices, and 'yes,' they were wrong, and many people were hurt, including you and your entire family."

"Start by asking God to forgive you so you can forgive yourself. That…Eleanor, you can control. Today was your first step toward your healing. Next is your family."

Eleanor's shoulders shook as she broke down, the weight of years of suppressed pain finally erupting. Dr. Riggio reached out her hand to console her, while handing her a Kleenex, resting gently on Eleanor's shoulder, reassuring her that things would be okay.

Eleanor let herself feel the full force of what she'd endured for the first time in years. The shame, the betrayal, the truth of her past—poured out in that small, quiet room. And though her heart ached, there was also the faintest glimmer of relief. Someone had finally heard *her*. Dr. Riggio had seen her pain and called it, what it was, *displacement* a name she had learned in one session.

"You may be right about displacement, Dr. Riggio. But where I'm from, you're either part of the solution or part of the problem. I sat quietly, enjoyed my lavish lifestyle, and turned a blind eye to his behavior.

That wasn't right." She looked at Dr. Riggio. "That makes me part of the problem." Eleanor released an odd chuckle as she wiped the tears from her face and reshaped her hair.

"What was that for?" Eleanor shrugged.

"I don't know. I feel like I should thank you for the extra time and session today. For years, I've felt trapped, and for the first time, I feel like maybe, just maybe, I can begin to reconnect with my family, church, and more importantly, me."

Dr. Riggio said, "Yes, Eleanor."

"Will you be my lifelong therapist? I have a lot more to unpack, and you can definitely handle my luggage."

"Of course, Eleanor," Dr. Riggio replied, and they smiled while they looked at each other, as Eleanor walked out of the office.

CHAPTER 11

A few days had passed since Gutter and his goons kidnapped Malcolm and threatened Clarence. After they were released and forced to find their way home, Malcolm left Clarence without saying a word. Clarence hadn't seen or heard from him until this cloudy Saturday morning.

While Clarence was asleep, Malcolm came over. He hoped he could get in and out without Clarence's knowledge, but his plan failed when his thoughts reconnected with his emotions—his rage caused him to yank clothes off hangers and slam drawers and closet doors while removing his clothes.

Clarence heard the loud noises from slamming the drawers, opening and closing in the guestroom. He instinctively grabbed the butcher knife he kept stashed under his pillow and jumped out of bed, running.

"I don't know who's in here, but whoever you are, I'm going to slice you until my arm hurts!" Clarence shouted aloud as he tiptoed toward the guest room. When he reached the bedroom door and peered inside, he lowered the knife and let out a long sigh of relief from the breath trapped in his chest.

Clarence stepped into the bedroom, his heart still pounding as he saw Malcolm hunched over an open suitcase, hurriedly tossing clothes inside. The closet door stood ajar, and shirts and pants were yanked from their hangers, some carelessly strewn across the floor. The normally composed Malcolm looked frantic, his movements sharp and agitated, far from his usual calm demeanor.

"Malcolm?" Clarence's voice trembled slightly as he stood frozen in the doorway, his hands gripping the doorframe. "What are you doing?"

Malcolm didn't stop. He shoved another shirt into the suitcase, the sound of the zipper grating as he forced the bag closed. "What does it look like, Clarence?" he muttered, barely glancing up. "I'm leaving."

Clarence's throat tightened, a deep pang of panic seizing his chest. He stepped closer, his voice low, pleading. "Leaving? What are you talking about? You can't just—"

"I can, and I am!" Malcolm's voice was firm, final. He snapped the suitcase shut and stood up, meeting Clarence's eyes for the first time. His face was tense, a mixture of exhaustion and frustration. "I didn't sign up for all this… insanity, Clarence!"

Clarence blinked, confused. "I don't understand—"

"Don't play dumb," Malcolm cut him off, his voice rising angrily. "This whole thing with you, Pastor Doug, Bishop Harrington, and Lord, the whole Harrington family! The constant games. The threats. Being *kidnapped* by Pastor Doug's goons, for Christ's sake!"

Clarence winced at the memory, his mind flashing back to seeing Malcolm bound and gagged in the back of that van. The pain he felt when Gutter twisted his ear and brought him to his knees. The feeling of the Glock muzzle kissing the back of his head. It had been terrifying, and Malcolm hadn't been the same since. But Clarence thought they would work through it together. He thought Malcolm understood why he couldn't just walk away from this fight, from exposing Doug—and his family—for the frauds he felt they were.

"Now you see why that family needs to be stopped. Kidnapping you is proof of what they are capable of doing, and getting away with it!"

"That's why I—This is exactly why I'm leaving!"

Malcolm moved past Clarence to grab his jacket, which hung in the closet near the door. "I can't do this anymore. Every day, it's something new—a new scheme, some new vendetta. I'm constantly looking over my shoulder, wondering if this is the day I get shot or abducted again just because I'm *with* you."

Clarence felt a deep ache in his chest, but he stepped closer, his voice trembling with emotion. "Malcolm, please. I need you. I can't do this alone."

Malcolm's eyes softened briefly, but his stern resolve quickly returned.

"You're not alone. You've got your revenge to keep you company." He sighed deeply, shaking his head. "I never signed up for this kind of drama, Clarence. I didn't expect to get dragged into some war between you and the church. I thought…" he paused, his voice breaking slightly, "…I thought we were building something normal, something real."

Clarence reached out, his index finger grazing Malcolm's arm, but Malcolm pulled back, the distance between them growing wider despite the small space.

"We *are* real, Malcolm," Clarence whispered. "I love you. I'm doing this for us. The Harringtons must be stopped. They are a family full of monsters."

Malcolm shook his head, his lips tight. "Maybe they are, but as long as you keep going after Pastor Doug, I'm a target! I'm not hanging around to possibly get killed because of your obsession with taking him…them…. down."

Clarence's heart raced, panic clawing at him. "It's not an obsession. It's justice. That family has ruined lives, Malcolm. They ruined my life."

"That's not true, and you know it! Pastor Doug hasn't done anything to you. You're angry at his dead father, and since you can't get to his dad, you're going after him. But here's what you forgot, Clarence…Pastor Doug wasn't always a pastor—he used to be a thug. I've got uncles who knew him from back in the day when "Pastor Doug" used to be out here in these streets robbing people. You ain't messin' with some nerdy pastor who don't know nothin' but the bible. You're messin' with a former goon who still has goons on speed dial. And it's clear to me, Clarence, that he's sick of you threatening him, his family, and his church. So, he sent his goons after you…and me." Malcolm grabbed the handle of the suitcase and lifted it off the bed. "You may be okay with that, but I ain't."

Malcolm's eyes were full of sadness, but they looked determined. It was clear to Clarence that this wasn't a fight he could win.

"I can't live like this, wondering every day if I'll make it home. I don't want to be caught in the crossfire of your war with the pastor of one of the biggest black churches in the city. I love you, but I won't die for you."

The words struck Clarence like a blow to the chest. He felt tears burning behind his eyes, but he blinked them away, his hands shaking as he tried to reach for Malcolm again.

"Please don't go," Clarence whispered. "I need you."

"Clarence, you don't need me; you need a counselor. And I ain't no psychiatrist." Malcolm gently touched Clarence's cheek. "I need to feel safe, Clarence. And with you, I don't…not anymore."

Malcolm's voice was soft, but its finality crushed Clarence's heart. He walked toward the door, his footsteps echoing in the room's silence.

Clarence stood frozen; the weight of his choices crashed down on him like a tidal wave. When the front door shut behind Malcolm, leaving Clarence alone in emptiness, the reality of what he'd lost settled like a stone in his chest.

Clarence's fingers curled. Both hands turned into fists. His brow scrunched, and the fire flickered in his eyes as he thought, *This ain't over, Pastor Doug...not by a long shot.*

CHAPTER 12

The church parking lot buzzed with energy as volunteers scurried about, preparing for the annual turkey giveaway. One week before Thanksgiving, the sky was cool with gray and light misty, foggy overcast. Despite the looming clouds, the air was thick with the promise of the Thanksgiving holiday—a mix of cold wind and the faint aroma of coffee filled the air.

Rows of folding tables stretched across the parking lot, each covered with boxes of canned goods, bags of potatoes, stuffing mix, and rows of freshly baked pies still steaming from local bakeries. Volunteers worked tirelessly, bundling each donation into neat packages while chatting and laughing, their voices a lively hum that filled the air. The tables were carefully organized, with signs overhead indicating the different sections—turkeys, pantry items, desserts—giving the event a sense of order amidst the busy preparations.

Bright, fluttering banners adorned the church's brick exterior, reading:

**The Annual Shekinah Holy Temple Thanksgiving
Community Blessing—Free Turkeys!**

A large tent erected near the entrance was filled with more supplies. The sides flapped gently in the wind as people bustled in and out, loading carts with food to bring to the main area.

A line of families had already formed along the edge of the parking lot despite the giveaway not officially starting for another hour. Mothers wrapped in thick scarves held their children's hands as they shuffled in place to keep warm. Older couples chatted quietly, clutching thermoses of coffee, while teenagers stood in clusters, joking and sharing earphones as they waited. The community had come together—those in need and those willing to give—forming an unspoken bond that made the chilly air feel slightly warmer.

Constance, William, and Pastor Doug stood surrounded by the volunteers near the center of the lot, going over last-minute details. Pastor Doug's warm, booming voice carried over the noise as he encouraged everyone to, "Remember the spirit of the season, that is… we are thankful, to be able, to give, this Thanksgiving! And let's make sure every family walk away feeling blessed."

"Let's pray, *Lord, we ask that you bless every family that will show up here today and that their needs will be met; we pray for every staff, volunteer, and leader who has given their time unselfishly to bless someone during this season of Thanksgiving! Holy Father, we thank you for blessing us to bless others, and Lord, we pray the humble prayer of thanksgiving over everyone who comes today in need or to bless someone in need according to your word in 1 Chronicles 16:34 because we believe that you are good and your love endures forever. In Jesus' name, we pray. AMEN!*"

"Now, let's get to work!"

He said loudly while rubbing his hands together with a huge smile.

Just behind the reverend, a group of teenagers helped unload the truck that was stacked high with frozen turkeys. They grunted and laughed as they handed off the heavy birds, each turkey wrapped in crisp, white paper, its cold surface sending a chill through their gloves. The clatter of crates and the thud of boxes hitting the ground filled the air as more deliveries arrived, trucks pulling up with their headlights beaming in the fading afternoon light.

Above all the movement, the church steeple stood tall, silhouetted against the dimming sky, its cross gleaming faintly as if watching over the scene below. The faint sound of gospel music drifted from the church's open doors, a peaceful background, to the hustle and bustle outside.

As the minutes ticked closer to the event's start, anticipation filled the air. Conversations quieted as families glanced toward the entrance, their eyes filled with hope and gratitude. Inside the church, tables were set for those staying after the giveaway for a warm meal while others prepared hot cocoa and cider to pass out to the waiting crowd.

The whole scene felt alive with purpose—an outpouring of generosity and community, the kind of spirit that made this small corner of the world feel like home, even to those who had so little. Despite the cold and clouds, there was warmth in every movement, every shared smile, and every turkey handed over with a blessing for the holiday to come.

In one corner, the children's choir sang familiar hymns, their melodies intertwining with the crowd's chatter. The atmosphere felt electric as stories were shared and laughter echoed, creating an unbreakable bond among the community.

As Katherine stood at the long table ready to serve those in line, the pre-made meals were being passed out at the other end of the parking lot. Her gloved hands carefully lifted containers of homemade frozen turkey dressing and passed them to the volunteers on her left.

The air around her was bustling, a mixture of laughter, chatter, and the occasional clang of metal pans being stacked. The cold breeze against her pale brown cheeks was flushed from the chilly air as she organized her station. She had overseen this part of the giveaway for years, perfecting the process as efficiently as possible.

Katherine moved with purpose, instructing the volunteers with calm authority. Each pan was portioned just right, labeled, and stacked neatly in the coolers to be passed out to the line of waiting families. She always prided herself on ensuring the turkey dressing was perfect—a blend of savory herbs, cornbread, and just the right amount of turkey drippings. It was the kind of dish that felt like love in every bite and comforted families in need.

"Okay, let's make sure each family gets one," Katherine said, tucking a stray strand of hair behind her ear as she scanned the table for any gaps in the setup. "We've got plenty, but let's stay organized."

As she handed another pan to a young volunteer, Katherine felt a sudden shift in the energy around her. The sound of footsteps crunching on the gravel behind her made her turn, and her heart skipped a beat when she did.

Standing a few feet away was Eleanor, her mother-in-law, and perhaps, in another life, Katherine's greatest nemesis. Eleanor's posture was as elegant and composed as always, her silver hair tucked neatly beneath a chocolate brown wool hat and her tan diamond quilted Burberry coat and black leather gloves. *Typical Eleanor*, Katherine pondered. The two women hadn't spoken more than a handful of words since the death of Eleanor's husband, Bishop Harrington. Their relationship had always been strained, marked by tension, unspoken judgments, and the undeniable fact that Eleanor had never truly liked her because of her unspoken reasons.

Eleanor's piercing eyes met Katherine's, and for a moment, neither woman spoke. Katherine's mind raced, trying to figure out what Eleanor could possibly want—there was no way she was here to help. Eleanor had long since stepped away from any church duties. And yet, here she was, standing in front of Katherine, of all places, in the busiest section of the giveaway.

Katherine cleared her throat, trying to mask her surprise. "Eleanor," she said evenly, forcing a polite smile. "I didn't expect to see you today."

To her credit, Eleanor returned the smile—though it was tighter and more reserved. She looked around at the bustling volunteers, the dressing trays, and the line of families waiting beyond.

"It's been a while since I've helped with a community event," she said, her voice soft but still carrying that undeniable air of authority. "I thought... maybe I could lend a hand. If there's room, of course."

Katherine blinked, taken aback. Of all the things she had expected— an awkward exchange, maybe even a sharp remark—*this* wasn't one of them. Eleanor offering to help? It felt strange, almost surreal, but Katherine could see the sincerity in her eyes, a vulnerability that hadn't been there in the past.

"Help?" Katherine echoed, her mind still trying to catch up. "I... well, yes, of course. We can always use an extra pair of hands."

Eleanor nodded, stepping closer to the table. Her movements were hesitant, as though she wasn't entirely sure where she fit in anymore. Eleanor had been a fixture in the church for so long—a woman of power and influence. But now, stripped of the title of First Lady and the status that had come with it, she was just... Eleanor. A widow. A mother. Someone who was trying to find her place once again.

Katherine handed her a pair of gloves, still feeling the awkward tension between them. "We're passing out the turkey dressing here," she explained, gesturing to the stacks of pans. "Each family gets one pan. It's frozen, but they can bake it at home for Thanksgiving."

Eleanor quickly removed her gloves and slipped on the white serving gloves. Her movements were deliberate as if she were testing the waters. "I see," she said softly, then looked at Katherine again, something softer in her gaze. "I know we've had... differences," she began, her voice low enough that only Katherine could hear. "But I've been thinking a lot lately and realize I could be doing more. For the church. For the people. For you."

Katherine wasn't sure how to respond. For so long, their relationship had been defined by those differences—Eleanor's quiet disapproval, the friction between them, the way Eleanor had always seemed to hold herself above, looking down on Katherine. But now, there was something different in Eleanor's eyes. A gesture of regret, perhaps something more straightforward—a desire to be useful or just part of something again.

"Well," Katherine said, after a moment of silence, "we could use your help. And since we are the backbone of the church…these families need both of *us*." She looked at Eleanor and smiled.

Eleanor's lips pressed into a thin smile, and she nodded. "Yes… they do."

The two women worked side by side, handing the frozen dressing to the waiting families. The awkwardness lingered, but with each passing minute, it seemed to lessen. Katherine could feel something shift between them—possibly unspoken forgiveness or an understanding of a quiet truce.

And though the gap between them was still wide, for the first time, it felt like maybe, *just* maybe, they were both willing to work on closing that gap.

CHAPTER 13

Pastor Doug stood amid the crowd, his presence warm and inviting. Dressed in a plaid flannel shirt and a wool beanie, he exuded joy and purpose. With a clipboard in hand, he called out instructions, his voice booming yet kind, resonating enthusiastically.

"Alright, everyone! Let's make sure we have enough bags ready for the families!" he encouraged as a group of volunteers stacked boxes filled with fresh produce and loaves of bread.

Children darted around, giggling and chasing one another, their laughter ringing like music. Some were tasked with decorating tables, while others filled colorful bags with cookies and treats. Nearby, a table laden with steaming hot cocoa and cider welcomed guests, adding to the cheerful atmosphere.

As the line of families began to form, Doug made his way down the queue, greeting each person with a warm handshake or a heartfelt hug.

"Happy Thanksgiving! We're so glad you're here!" he said, his eyes sparkling with genuine joy.

The organized and spirited volunteers moved efficiently, handing out turkeys in festive paper bags with fresh vegetables and other dinner sides. Each recipient was left with food, smiles, laughter, love, and a sense of belonging.

As the sun climbed higher in the sky, casting a golden glow over the church, Pastor Doug gathered everyone for a brief moment of gratitude. With hands clasped and heads bowed, he offered a prayer, his voice steady and hopeful.

"Thank you for this day, for the abundance we share, and for this community that supports one another," he said.

When he finished the prayer, the crowd applauded. The reaction was a testament to their shared spirit and togetherness. With hearts full and bellies soon to be satisfied, they continued their work, each turkey a symbol of generosity, love, and the true essence of the giving of Thanksgiving.

Suddenly, the festive atmosphere shifted. The crowd parted like the Red Sea. Clarence stumbled into view. His hair looked like it hadn't come close to a comb in weeks. His clothes were disheveled. His eyes, bloodshot and unfocused, darted around the crowd before landing on Pastor Doug. In one hand, he had a bottle of whiskey. His other hand was directed at Pastor Doug, his index finger shooting like an arrowhead.

"Hey! You!" Clarence shouted and slurred, raising his voice above the cheerful chatter. "I know what you're hiding!"

A hush fell over the crowd as heads turned toward him, instantly dampening Pastor Doug's jovial spirit. His expression changed from warmth to concern as he stepped forward, attempting to defuse the situation.

"Clarence, let's talk about this," he said calmly, extending a hand in a gesture of peace.

But Clarence wasn't having it.

"You think you can keep all your secrets safe? I know what goes on behind those doors!" he shouted, stumbling closer. "I'll tell everyone! You're not so righteous, after all!" He looked at Constance, his ex-wife, and shook his head in disgust. "And look at you…still scared to live your truth. Around here fakin' it…livin' for your family instead of yourself."

Constance's hand shook violently. The urge to slap the taste out of Clarence's mouth was at an all-time high. But her eyes said something different. They were filled with sorrow and regret. They pleaded with Clarence to leave before something bad happened to him.

"This isn't the place or time for this," Constance whispered to the man she'd been pressured to marry and at one time considered her closest friend.

Clarence pointed his finger at Constance's face. "You don't get to tell me what to do. No more!" He glared at Pastor Doug. "And neither do you. You're just as shady and lowdown as your daddy was!"

Murmurs rippled through the crowd, a mix of shock and confusion. Security personnel, who had been stationed discreetly nearby, sprang into action. Two men approached Clarence, their expressions serious but non-threatening.

"Sir, you need to calm down. It is time to leave," one of them said firmly, stepping in front of him. "Let's get you some help."

"No! I'm not going anywhere!" Clarence yelled, backing away but losing his balance and teetering. "They're all just sheep, following him blindly! I won't let you—"

"Don't just stand there!" William shouted. "Take him away!"

In a swift motion, the security team moved in, grasping Clarence's arms to steady him.

"We're going to escort you off the property," the second officer said, maintaining a steady grip.

The crowd watched in concern and disbelief as Clarence struggled, his voice rising in protest. "You can't silence me! I know what you're doing, Doug! You're a fraud!"

With a final tug, the security team led him away, his protests fading into the distance.

As the tension in the air began to settle, Pastor Doug took a deep breath, his demeanor still calm despite the chaos.

"I want to assure everyone that we are here for each other, and we will continue to support one another," he said, trying to recapture the moment. "Let's focus on the good we're doing today. This is a time for gratitude and community."

Slowly, the crowd began to relax, conversations picking up again, though the unease lingered. Pastor Doug exchanged concerned glances with a few members, knowing that the day's events would weigh heavily on their hearts. But he was determined to remind them of their purpose, of the love that united them all.

Once the chaos subsided and everyone refocused on why they'd all gathered, Pastor Doug attempted to retreat to his office.

"Doug!" Katherine called out.

Pastor Doug stopped in his tracks and turned around.

"Honey, are you okay?"

"Sweetheart, I'm fine."

"Are you sure? I've never seen Clarence act like that."

"He was drunk," Doug said.

"Clearly! What got into him?"

"Based on that liquor bottle he was holding, I'd say spirits got into him." He gently kissed Katherine's lips. "Now, I need you to go back out there and help get everyone back to serving the families while I go to my office and try to regain my composure."

Katherine nodded in agreement.

Doug kissed her cheek and whispered, "Thank you."

Once inside his office, Pastor Doug closed the door behind him and punched at the air while struggling to suppress a growl. After a few seconds of beating up the air, he remembered something—the burner phone Gutter gave him. He retrieved the phone from his desk drawer and made a call.

After a few rings, Gutter picked up, his voice gruff but steady. "What's going on, Pastor?"

"Gutter!" Doug said, his voice low and urgent.

"What's up, Dougie? What has happened, man?"

"It's about Clarence. He just made a scene at the turkey giveaway, threatening to expose me and the church."

There was a brief silence on the other end before Gutter responded, a hint of anger creeping into his tone. "Clarence just showed up there?"

"Yeah. He just came here stinkin' drunk and called me out in front of about two hundred people. I thought you were goin' to handle this."

"I thought I did."

"Well, clearly, you didn't scare him enough because he showed up here raising hell. The guy has become unpredictable." Doug admitted, running a hand through his hair. "I'm worried he might escalate things."

"Don't worry, Pastor. I'll deal with him once and for all," Gutter said, his voice firm and unwavering. "I'll make sure he understands the consequences of his actions. No more threats. No more games."

"Okay...Just... be careful," Pastor Doug urged, anxiety gnawing at him. "I don't want any trouble, especially not in our church. We're trying to build trust, not fear."

Gutter chuckled darkly. "Trust me, Pastor. I know how to keep things quiet. Just focus on your flock. Leave the messy stuff to me."

Pastor Doug sighed, feeling a mixture of relief and unease. "Thank you, Gutter. I just want to protect our church and the good we're doing here."

"I got your back, Doug. Always," Gutter replied. "I'll take care of it."

With a final exchange of reassurances, Doug hung up. He put the burner phone back in the drawer and then took a moment to gather himself, staring out the window at the parking lot where the event had just taken place. He knew he had to stay focused on the event, but the weight of Clarence's threats lingered in the back of his mind.

As he composed himself, he silently vowed to confront whatever darkness lay ahead, determined to shield his congregation and family from harm. He was taking a deep breath to calm himself when he heard a light knock at the door.

"I'll be out in a second!"

A few seconds passed, there was another light tap on the door.

Doug marched toward the door. "I said give me a—"

His words were clipped when he opened the door and saw his mother.

"Mama, I'm sorry, I didn't know it was you."

"I know you didn't," Eleanor said calmly.

"I just need a few minutes to get myself together."

"I know you do," Eleanor said and barged in, "which is why I won't take too much of your time saying what I need to say."

Doug closed the door after his mother entered.

"Mama, I—"

Eleanor held up her hand. "Son, be quiet and listen to me. You may be the head of this church, but I'm still your mama."

"Yes, ma'am," Pastor Doug said sheepishly.

"I saw what happened in the parking lot. How are you doing?"

"Clarence has become unhinged. He—"

Eleanor raised her hand again, signaling him to stop talking. "I didn't ask about Clarence because I already know what he's upset about."

"You do?"

"Son, I've been here since your father started this church. I know where all the bodies are buried…figuratively speaking. Clarence suffers from a case of displaced aggression. He's angry at your father, but since your father is dead, he's transferred that spirit to you."

"Mom, I have no idea what Daddy promised him other than money. For all I know, Clarence could be making stuff up."

Eleanor nodded. "Maybe he is," she shrugged, "maybe he's not because a lot of things were promised to him in exchange for his silence. Unfortunately, your father is dead, and Clarence realizes that he won't get what he was promised unless you agree to it. Let me guess…Clarence came to talk to you at some point, and you told him all deals were off?"

Pastor Doug nodded and thought, *Man, she's good.* "As much as I hate to admit it, I've been feeling so overwhelmed with everything that's been happening: trying to get acclimated to this position, church drama, community drama, and all this family drama. People are fighting, anger is everywhere, and it's tearing us apart…tearing me apart," he admitted as he lowered and rubbed his head.

Eleanor nodded with empathy in her eyes. "It's a challenging time, that's for sure." She stepped closer, her voice firm yet passionate. "I've been thinking about what the scripture says in Deuteronomy 20:4, *'For the LORD your God is the one who goes with you to fight for you against your enemies to give you victory.'* (NIV)."

"Sometimes that's hard…even for a pastor."

"You don't have to tell me. I know that all too well. But this is a scripture I memorized long ago— before our lives became so complex and convoluted." Eleanor closed her eyes tight and recalled the scripture.

"For we do not wrestle against flesh and blood, but against the rulers, against the authorities, against the cosmic powers over this present darkness, against the spiritual forces of evil in the heavenly places."

"Ephesians 6:12," Pastor Doug said as his eyes lit up. "A powerful reminder that our battles are not always what they seem."

Eleanor opened her eyes, turned toward her son, and said, "Exactly. If we keep fighting each other, we'll never find peace. We must trust that God will handle the bigger fight for us."

"You're right, Mama."

"I know I am." Eleanor walked over to her son and gently held him at arm's length. "Look, your daddy built this church from nothing. Along the way, he and his sidekicks hurt many people—Clarence was one of those people. I can admit that I sat idle and did nothing to stop the madness—that makes me complicit. That's a harsh reality I must live with, but you don't."

"Now, God has elevated you to the position you are in. Not your sister. Not your brother. Not me." She pointed at Doug. "God appointed you to lead this congregation. And last I checked, our God doesn't make mistakes. No man—not even Clarence—can take away from you what God has called you to do. So, it would be best if you didn't take matters into your own hands. Remember, the battle is not yours. Turn this issue with Clarence over to the Lord. Set a vision and a path for this church and lead us toward it. And I want you to be unapologetic about it. You don't owe anyone an explanation for what you decide to do as the Pastor of this church. The moment you start seeking the approval of your flock, your flock will start expecting you to run things past them before you make decisions...and that's not how the job is done. Your daddy may have been flawed, but there was no doubt about who was in charge."

"You're right about that."

Eleanor affectionately touched Doug's chin and forced him to look into her eyes. "I know you can do this."

"Thanks, Mama."

"That's all the preaching I'm gon' do today. I gotta get back out there and help Katherine pass out this food."

After Eleanor left, the sudden quietness of his office enveloped him like a protective cloak. His mother's words rang in his ear. Instantly, he knew she had been used to convey God's word.

"I hear you, Lord," Pastor Doug mumbled.

He walked over to the mini-refrigerator in the corner of his office, grabbed a bottle of water, and took a swig like a thirsty athlete. Mid-gulp, he remembered his call to Gutter.

As frustrated as I am with Clarence, I can't let Gutter hurt him, Doug thought.

He placed the water bottle on the fridge and quickly returned to his desk to retrieve the burner phone. His hands trembled slightly as he dialed Gutter. That nervous energy increased when, over the next ten minutes, the five times he dialed the number, Gutter didn't answer.

Doug slid the phone back into his pocket. He stared aimlessly out the window as images of a drunk and emotional Clarence clashing with a heartless criminal like Gutter scrolled across his mind.

Oh my God, Pastor Doug thought. *I've got to get to Clarence before Gutter does.*

CHAPTER 14

Clarence sat slumped on the couch. It had barely been an hour since Pastor Doug's security team escorted him off the church property and tossed him onto the hood of his car parked across the street.

"I'll kill you if you touch me again!" was the last verbal barrage Clarence managed to fire in the direction of the security staff before they disappeared.

His biceps burned, and his shoulder joint smarted something fierce. Clarence rubbed his shoulder at the joint to make sure it was still attached to his torso. The pain would have been more immense had he not been so "liquored" up.

It was a miracle that he made it to his apartment safely because the journey back was like navigating an obstacle course. While driving with blurred vision and a strong desire to vomit, he ran two red lights, swerved into oncoming traffic, and nearly side-swiped a parked SUV. They honked excessively. He responded to all of his protesters with a middle finger held high.

It'd been said that the police were never around when you needed them—the woman pushing a baby stroller had to run across an intersection to keep from being hit by Clarence's erratic driving and probably thought that very thing! He sped up vigorously and sharply turned the V-shaped corner with his BMW on two wheels, turning onto his street. Fortunately, the entry gate to his apartment complex was open. Otherwise, he most certainly would have rammed right into it.

Clarence managed to park without sideswiping any of his neighbor's vehicles. It wasn't the type of parking that would have passed a driving test—his vehicle straddled two spaces—but he managed to do it without hurting the car, himself, or anyone who happened to be within five feet of him. After staggering to his first-floor apartment, Clarence fumbled with his keys until he found the one that fit his lock. When Clarence turned the key, the door flew open, and he fell onto the floor.

"Home sweet home," he muttered and laughed.

Clarence crawled to his sofa. The whiskey bottle he toted onto the church grounds fell from his hand and shattered when the security guards snatched him like a rag doll. But Clarence didn't miss it because a bottle of Cognac was sitting on his coffee table. He grabbed it, ripped off the top, took a hearty swig, and collapsed on the sofa.

Although it was a little past six o'clock in the evening, his apartment was dimly lit because he kept the drapes closed. It felt cold, hollow—so much quieter without Malcolm's presence to fill it.

"Malcolm, Malcolm, Maalllcollmmm!"

Clarence removed his cell phone from his pocket. His vision was blurred, not just from the alcohol, but from the frustration and the ache that had settled deep into his bones since Malcolm had walked out.

"I'm gon' get you back," Clarence slurred. "That family has already ruined my life. I'm not about to let 'em ruin my relationship with you too!"

Clarence tapped the button to dial Malcolm and then pressed the phone tightly to his ear. The phone rang endlessly on the other end, and Clarence's head throbbed with each unanswered ring. He was so drunk that he wasn't even sure how long he'd been calling—minutes, hours? It didn't matter. He needed to hear Malcolm's voice and somehow make him understand that he couldn't lose him…not like this.

Finally, Clarence heard the familiar sound of Malcolm's voicemail. The recorded voice, warm and steady, sounded so far away now:

Hey, it's Malcolm. You know what to do.

The tone beeped, and for a moment, Clarence just sat there, his mouth dry, his heart racing in his chest. He brought the bottle to his lips, taking another long swig before slamming it back onto the table. The liquor burned its way down, but it wasn't enough to dull the ache in his chest.

"*Malcolm,*" Clarence slurred into the phone, his voice cracking with desperation. "*It's me. I need you to call me back. Please, I'm begging you.*" He stopped, his thoughts swimming, words slipping away as quickly as they formed. "*I don't know what to say. I just…I need you. I need you to come back. I know I've messed things up. I know I haven't…been the easiest to love, but you can't just walk out like this. Not after everything we've been through.*"

He paused and wiped his mouth with the back of his hand. His thoughts flashed back to their last conversation, to Malcolm standing in the bedroom with that look of finality on his face. It had gutted him.

"*Look,*" Clarence continued, his voice cracking, "*I get it. I know things have been crazy. And maybe I haven't protected you the way I should have. But…but I'm trying. I'm really trying. I'm just…I'm so lost without you, Mal. Please…just come home. We can figure it out. We can fix this.*"

Clarence wiped a tear from his cheek, his mind clouded with the haze of whiskey and regret. He was losing Malcolm. The realization crashed over him again and again, relentless, suffocating.

His voice grew quieter, trembling with the weight of his words. "*I love you. I love you so much and can't do this without you.*"

There was only silence on the other end. Just the emptiness of the voicemail, the cold reminder that Malcolm wasn't going to pick up. That he wasn't coming home.

Clarence exhaled shakily, the pain in his chest tightening. His hand gripped the phone until his knuckles turned white. *"Malcolm..."* he whispered, his voice barely audible. *"Please don't leave me. I...I..."* Clarence's train of thought was derailed when he heard something fall to the floor in his bedroom. "What was that?" he asked as if talking to a human on the phone, not a recording device designed to relay a message. *"I don't know who else to turn to. I think someone is crawling through my bedroom window."* He heard another loud noise. That's when he stood up and whispered. *"I've gotta go. I think someone just broke in here. Just remember...I love you."*

Clarence lowered the phone from his ear as he stared blankly at the hallway leading to his bedroom. His fight-or-flight instincts had come alive. However, he knew he was too drunk to put up a good fight or run. His only option was to stay put and try to think of what to do. He was confused and scared.

For a moment, the only sound in the room was the steady ticking of the clock on the wall. Its rhythmic click cut through the still and quiet room, an agonizing reminder of the time slipping away. After a few seconds passed, nothing happened. He no longer heard anything threatening.

"I'm so drunk, I'm starting to hear things," he mumbled and waved dismissively at the perceived threat.

After he sat back down, he was about to take another drink but froze when something caught his attention—a faint noise from the bedroom. Clarence frowned, his drunken mind slow to process it at first.

Now, I know I heard something that time, he thought and squinted at the hallway leading to his bedroom.

He leaned forward slightly, listening. It was soft, barely audible over the pounding in his head, but it was there. A cracking sound. Footsteps, maybe? Or the scrape of something against the door?

His heart skipped a beat, and he sat up straighter, his senses sharpening despite the alcohol in his system. *What the hell was that?*

For a moment, there was only silence. Then, the unmistakable sound of the doorknob jiggling.

Clarence's blood ran cold. He put the bottle down slowly and looked at the front door. He wanted to gauge whether he could reach the front door before the intruder made it to him.

The knob rattled again, this time more forcefully. Someone had come to get him.

The fog of his drunken haze cleared just enough for panic to set in. He reached for his phone again, but his hands were shaking too much to dial anything. His eyes darted around the room, searching for something—anything—that he could use to defend himself.

The knob rattled once more, followed by a soft click. Clarence's breath hitched. His fight-or-flight instincts were on high alert, but again he missed his opportunity window. The bedroom door opened slowly, and the figure stepped into the room, the outline barely visible in the dim light.

"Who the hell—"

"Remember me, Clarence?" said Gutter as he moved from the shadows of the bedroom hallway and into the living room. "I'm the dude who told you to stay away from Pastor Doug." Gutter pulled out a prison-style shank from the pocket of his black hoodie. "Since you didn't take heed, you give me no choice but to show you that I mean business."

Clarence's voice broke. His throat was dry with fear. His brain directed him to respond, but before the words could pass his lips, Gutter moved closer, quick, silent, and deliberate. And then…everything went dark.

CHAPTER 15

The sun hung low in the sky, casting long shadows across the church parking lot as Pastor Doug sprinted toward his car. His breath came in quick bursts, and he could almost taste the freedom of a quiet evening at home. Just as he reached the driver's side, he heard his brother William's voice call out.

"Doug! Wait up!" William shouted.

Doug turned, his heart sinking as he spotted William and Constance striding toward him, concern etched on their faces.

"Is everything okay?" William asked, his brow furrowed. "We should've arrested that fool instead of just tossing him off the church grounds."

"What's going on?" Constance added, her voice tinged with urgency. "Where are you rushing off to, Dougie?"

Doug may have been the pastor, but he was still just Dougie to his siblings—especially when no church members were around to hear their discussions. But just because it was only the three of them standing in that tight huddle, it didn't mean they weren't being watched by church members who'd witnessed Clarence's outburst.

"Look, I really can't talk about it right now," Doug said, glancing nervously at the parking lot exit. "It's complicated."

"Complicated?" Constance said quizzically.

"So, you're just gonna leave in the middle of this important event?" William asked.

"Dougie, we're family," Constance said. "If you're in trouble, let us help."

Doug's voice cracked slightly, and he ran a hand through his hair, frustration bubbling beneath the surface. "Thanks, Cee, but I got this."

"You can't just shut us out!" William said angrily. "We may not be the pastor, but we're high-ranking leaders of this church, and we deserve to know what's going on."

"I'm not shutting you out! I just... I don't have all the answers yet."

"You can call it what you want, but it's obvious that something bad is going down, and we have a right to know," William said. "You can't just leave us hanging like this!"

Doug was about to explain, but his mother's words came to mind, *"You don't owe anyone an explanation for the things you decide to do as the head of this church. The moment you start seeking the approval of your flock, your flock will start expecting you to run things past them before you make decisions...and that's not how the job is done."*

"I can, and I am," Doug fired back. "Where I'm going is not important to y'all. Constance, what I need you to do while I'm gone is make sure all the volunteers get breaks and have time to eat. We're not running a plantation." He pointed at his brother. "Will, I need you to speak to the Chief of Police and Fire Marshall. They both will be making their appearance today, and you know they would like nothing else than to shut us down and make a show while doing it. William, be the church's spokesperson in my absence—make sure the crowd is controlled and no one is gathering at the exits obstructing traffic flow. Now, if it's too much responsibility for you, I'll put someone else in charge." He took a moment to catch his breath and then looked at Constance. "I'll be back in an hour or so."

"Go do what you gotta do, Pastor," Constance said and smiled.

Doug winked at his sister, kissed her on the cheek, and sprinted away.

William looked like he'd been whacked upside the head with a bag of nickels. William and Constance watched Doug run away.

"The power has gone to his head," William mumbled. "I don't know who he thinks he is."

"He's our pastor," Constance barked and looked at William with annoyance. "And you need to do what he told you to do."

CHAPTER 16

Malcolm entered his tiny apartment, the door clicking shut behind him with a familiar thud. The dim light from the overhead bulb illuminated the cluttered space—books stacked haphazardly, a laundry basket overflowing in the corner. He took a deep breath, trying to shake off the anxiety that clung to him like a shadow.

He moved to the small kitchen, the cool tiles beneath his feet a welcome contrast to the heat of the moment. Rummaging through the fridge, he grabbed a cold Dr. Pepper, unscrewing the bottle cap with a shaky hand. As he took a long sip, he could still hear Clarence's voice echoing in his mind, the urgency in every word.

Malcolm leaned against the counter, feeling the coolness of the bottle against his forehead for a moment. He needed to recalibrate and find some calm before returning to the chaos of the outside world.

He closed his eyes and took a deep breath, savoring the crisp taste of the soda as he drank, but it wasn't enough to quiet the storm inside him.

Setting the bottle down, he glanced at the clock—it felt like time had slowed, each tick amplifying his worry.

With a heavy sigh, he reached into his bag, pulled out his phone, and saw that Clarence had called numerous times. His phone had been on vibrate, so he missed his calls. He rubbed the back of his neck, tension coiling tightly. Should he listen to the voice messages that Clarence has left or delete them? Before he knew it, his thumb was moving toward the delete button. Just as he was about to delete the last message, a little voice told him to listen to it—so he did.

Malcolm stood as stiff as a mannequin in the kitchen with his cell phone cradled in the palm of his hand and stared at the screen while he replayed the voicemail for what felt like the hundredth time. The familiar beep signaled the start of Clarence's pitiful message.

Malcolm, it's me again. I need you to call me back. Please, I'm begging you...

Clarence's voice trembled, a mix of fear and urgency that sent a chill down Malcolm's spine.

As the voicemail continued, Malcolm's heart raced. He could hear the tremors in Clarence's voice, the way words spilled out.

Something's wrong. I think someone's—

Malcolm's pulse quickened. He leaned closer, straining to catch every word. His mind raced as he replayed the message again, and when he heard the call ended abruptly and really thought about what Clarence said, it hit him...

"It may be those guys who kidnapped me," Malcolm mumbled as a chill raced down his spine.

Malcolm's fingers shook as he quickly dialed 911, his heart pounding like a drum in his ears. As the phone rang, he glanced around his quiet room, the stillness contrasting sharply with Clarence's fear.

"911, what's your emergency?" The operator's voice cut through the tension.

"I—I need to report a possible break-in," Malcolm stammered, trying to keep his voice steady. "My friend, he's in his apartment and thinks someone is inside with him! I just listened to his voicemail... he's scared."

"Can you give me your friend's address?" the operator asked, her tone calm but firm.

Malcolm recited the address, his thoughts racing. "He might be in danger! Please, hurry!"

"Help is on the way," she assured him. "Stay on the line with me until they arrive. Can you describe your friend?"

Malcolm swallowed hard, trying to focus. "Clarence... he's slim, 5'9", about 165 pounds, light brown complexion, and wears glasses. He... he's shaken up. I just don't know what to do."

"Just breathe, sir. Help will be there shortly. Is there any way for you to contact him directly?"

"No! He won't pick up. He's scared!"

Malcolm's voice cracked, desperation creeping in.

"Stay calm. I'll keep you updated," the operator said.

As Malcolm held the phone pressed against his ear, his palm sweety, he felt the weight of the situation crash down on him. He paced the room, anxiously glancing at his phone, half-hoping for a message from Clarence, half-dreading what he might hear.

The silence felt oppressive, and all he could do was wait, praying the police would get to his friend before it was too late.

CHAPTER 17

Pastor Doug smartly parked his car a block from Clarence's apartment complex. He hopped out and sprinted toward the apartments, his heart racing with every step. Aware that his face might be recognized, he pulled the hood of his hoodie over his head and slowed to a brisk walk as he approached the entrance.

When the gate opened, and a car exited, Doug slithered inside the complex.

Please be okay, he thought as he approached the door to Clarence's apartment, his breath coming in quick gasps. That thought became audible as he reached for the doorknob.

"Please be okay," he whispered and knocked.

When no one answered, he reached for the doorknob, hoping that with any luck, it might be unlocked—it was. Doug opened the front door, the hinges creaking ominously. The apartment was eerily quiet, and the silence caused his anxiety to spike.

"Clarence?" he called out, stepping inside.

The living room was dimly lit, shadows pooling in the corners. Everything seemed in place—except for Clarence, who was not anywhere in sight. His heart thudding in his chest, Pastor Doug moved further in, glancing around.

"Clarence! It's Doug!" Panic began to creep in as he saw no sign of the man who—at least on paper—was still his brother-in-law.

The air felt thick and heavy with an unspoken tension. Then, out of the corner of his eye, he spotted a door slightly ajar at the end of the hallway. He hurried toward it with a mix of dread and determination, each step echoing in the stillness.

"Clarence!" he called again, more urgent this time.

Pastor Doug pushed the door open wider. The sight that met his eyes sent a jolt of terror through his veins. There was Gutter, sitting on the edge of the bed, covered in blood.

"Gutter! Where is Clarence?"

Gutter jutted his head to the closet. Doug rushed over to the closet and saw Clarence's bloody body stuffed inside the tiny space like a pretzel. Next to him, on the floor, was the six-inch shank that Gutter used.

"No, no, no!"

Pastor Doug cried out and dropped to his knees. He reflexively grabbed Clarence and tried to drag his body out of the closet, but the giant standing behind him halted his momentum.

Gutter reached down and grabbed Pastor Doug around the waist. He pulled the pastor back into the center of the bedroom.

"I need to check for a pulse, Gutter; he may still be alive!"

Gutter hit Pastor Doug in the chest with a stiff arm. The blow made him stagger backward.

"No! What you need to do is get the hell out of here!"

"I can't leave him like this."

"It's too late to save him."

Doug reached down and planted his hands on his knees like a runner who was out of breath. Without looking up, he said, "I never wanted him dead, Gutter."

"I know."

"Then why'd you kill him?"

"Because when he came after you—after I told him not to—in front of my crew, he killed my rep. And you know how it is out there in dem streets…a man's rep is all he got. If I didn't deal with Clarence, people in my crew would think I've gotten soft. Before you know it, they'd start challenging me…and I can't have that."

"But—"

"But, nothin' Dougie! I did what I had to do."

Gutter staggered backward dizzily. His big body smacked the wall, and he slumped as if he slid down the wall. Doug moved closer.

"Gutter, is this Clarence's blood or your own?"

Gutter smirked. "Probably a lil bit of both. That little sissy was drunk and still put up a fight." He shook his head in disgust. "Back in the day, I would've finished him off in seconds. I'm glad my days are numbered. I don't know how much longer this lion can last in the jungle."

"What's that supposed to mean? All this blubber, a little knife wound ain't gon' kill you."

"I wish it was something as simple as a knife wound, bruh."

"What are you sayin', Gee?"

"Time ain't on my side, Rev."

Pastor Doug's brow furrows, sensing a deeper truth.

"What do you mean?"

Gutter looked at Pastor Doug. The bravado that had become his armor started to fade away.

"I got diagnosed with Stage 4 pancreatic cancer. Doctors gave me a few months, maybe six…eight, who knows."

The confession hit Pastor Doug so hard that he nearly forgot about the dead body in the closet. Suddenly, he nodded as if hit with a revelation. "It's all starting to make sense."

"I figured you'd catch on," Gutter said.

"That's why you've been so willing to get in the middle of this beef."

"Better me than you. You've got too much to lose. I'm not worried about jail or anything else. I won't be around to go to trial."

Pastor Doug shook his head, struggling to find the right words.

"I can't let you go out like this, Gee. You can still turn things around, seek forgiveness, find peace—Oh my God, what have I done? Gutter!"

"Peace? I don't have time for peace, but you did what you had to do, Doug. I've spent my life in these streets, and somehow karma has come back around."

Gutter looked away; his tough exterior cracked for a moment.

Pastor Doug stepped closer, hoping to reach him. "You don't have to face this alone. There's still hope, even in the darkest moments. Let me help you get out of here, we can both go."

"Hope? Nah, dog, I've seen too much to believe in that anymore."

Pastor Doug took a deep breath and searched for the right words. "You may think your story is over, but it doesn't have to end like this. You can still make choices that matter, brother."

Gutter finally met Pastor Doug's gaze, a flicker of vulnerability was in his eyes.

"Why should I?" Gutter asked, fighting back tears.

"Because even with limited time, you can leave a legacy. You can choose to make it your life meaningful, not just about anger or revenge."

Gutter jutted his head over to the closet. "It's too late, Rev." Gutter's facade began to crumble.

"It's never too late, my brotha."

Gutter smiled. "You know when I first heard you'd become a pastor, I thought it was all fake." He pointed at Doug. "You know we've been down for years."

"Down like four flat tires."

"I knew you when you were out here in these streets robbing people, Doug."

"I can't deny it…that was me."

"I know it was you because I was right there with you." Gutter started coughing uncontrollably. Once he regained his composure, he finished. "But once I heard you preach—"

"Wait, you heard me preach?"

"Yeah, I had to see for myself. I snuck into the church to listen to one of your sermons." He smiled and nodded. "You got skills, dude."

Gutter held up his fist. Doug made a fist and gave him a bump.

Their *moment* was interrupted by the sound of police sirens.

"That's your cue to leave, Rev."

"I ain't leavin' you, Gee."

"You'd better get the hell out of here while you can."

Pastor Doug fought back tears and shook his head.

"Dougie, you have a wife, kids, and a church full of people who hang on to your every word. I have six months to live…if I'm lucky. Don't mess up your life, bruh." He jutted his head toward the window. "Go out the way I came in."

The sirens grew closer.

"Dougie, I ain't never begged no one for anything. Don't make me beg you to leave. I knew what I was doing when I came here." He winced and grabbed his stomach. "You asked me why I did it. I'll tell you why. I killed that fool because I didn't want him to ruin the realest brotha I know." Gutter took a deep breath and said, "Get out of here…please."

Pastor Doug stepped back and took one last look at the man who had protected him when he was ripping and running the streets, behind prison bars, and as a pastor—he was a real one!

"God bless you, brotha, true brothers till the end! Love you."

Pastor Doug whispered and crawled out the bedroom window.

CHAPTER 18

Doug stood in the bathroom, gripping the edges of the sink as he stared into the mirror. His reflection was pale and haunted, the dark circles under his eyes contrasting his typically composed face. His chest rose and fell in shallow breaths, and for a moment, he didn't recognize the man staring back at him.

Blood was smeared across his hands, dried in places where he hadn't wiped it away. His hoodie—once a soft, comfortable gray—was splattered with dark, crusted patches, the smell of iron clinging to him like a suffocating cloud. His jeans were no better, stained in streaks that sent a chill down his spine every time he glanced at them.

He didn't know how long he had stood there, frozen, trying to force himself to move. Every inch of his body felt heavy, like the weight of the night was pressing him into the earth, pulling him down. His mind buzzed, replaying fragments of what had happened, but he quickly shut them out. He couldn't think about it…not now.

With trembling hands, he turned on the faucet, watching as the water sputtered to life, the stream cold before warming. Slowly, he brought his hands under it, scrubbing at the blood that had seeped into his skin. The water turned pink, swirling down the drain as he worked, but no matter how much he washed, he couldn't shake the feeling the blood was still there, still staining him. He scrubbed harder, his hands growing raw.

When he couldn't take it anymore, Doug turned the water off, peeled off the hoodie, and tossed it onto the bathroom floor with a wet thud. The jeans followed, crumpled in a heap beside it. His breath came out in shaky gasps as he stared at the pile of clothes—*evidence*, he thought. The remnants of a night that had spiraled out of control. A night he wished he could erase.

He gathered the bundle of fabric, his movements automatic now, like he was moving through a fog. His bare feet padded softly down the hallway as he entered the living room toward the fireplace. The room was dark except for the faint glow of the streetlights seeping through the curtains. The house felt eerily still, as if it knew something terrible had happened, too.

Doug knelt in front of the fireplace, his hands moving mechanically as he set the hoodie and jeans inside. For a moment, he hesitated, staring at the pile. The blood on the clothes seemed darker now, like a shadow in the dim light. He swallowed hard, then grabbed the lighter from the mantle.

The flame flickered to life, casting a soft orange glow on his face as he held it to the edge of the hoodie. Slowly, the fabric began to catch, the fire spreading, crackling as it consumed the clothes. The smell of burning cotton filled the room, thick and acrid, but Doug didn't move. He watched as the flames grew, the heat brushing against his skin, burning away the evidence of what he had done.

When the last fabric turned to ash, Doug collapsed onto the couch, his body sinking into the cushions. The adrenaline had worn off, leaving behind a bone-deep exhaustion that made his limbs feel like lead. He closed his eyes, rubbing his temples as if that would chase away the growing ache in his head, but the weight of what he'd done sat heavy in his chest, suffocating him.

Pastor Doug's inside voice kept repeating, *What have you done?*

A soft click echoed through the house. The front door opened and closed, and Doug's heart skipped a beat—it was Katherine. She stepped into the living room, her eyes immediately finding him slumped and defeated on the couch. She paused in the doorway, taking in the scene—the faint smell of smoke lingering in the air, the hollowness in his eyes. Her face softened, concern washing over her like a wave.

"Doug?" She called softly, stepping closer. "What's going on? What happened?"

He didn't answer; he just kept his eyes closed and his jaw clenched tight. The silence between them stretched thick with unspoken words. He couldn't tell her. He couldn't put the nightmare of tonight into words. The guilt, the fear, the blood… it was all too much. He wasn't even sure he could make sense of it himself.

Katherine knelt beside him, placing a gentle hand on his knee. He flinched at the contact but didn't pull away. She could feel the tension in his muscles, the way his body seemed to hold everything in like he was teetering on the edge of breaking.

"Doug," she whispered, her voice tender but firm. "Please talk to me. I know something's wrong."

He opened his eyes, then blinking down at her, his vision blurry with exhaustion and something else—something raw and broken. Tears welled up, threatening to spill, and for a moment, he couldn't speak. All he could do was look at her, his wife, the one person he had tried so hard to protect from the darkness that now clung to him like a second skin.

"I can't," he rasped, his voice barely above a whisper. "I can't, Kat."

Katherine's brow furrowed, her eyes shining with worry and fear for him. She knew something terrible had happened—she could see it in the way his body sagged, in the haunted look in his eyes—but she didn't push. Instead, she slid onto the couch beside him, wrapping her arms around him, pulling him close.

Doug's body stiffened initially, but something inside him broke as her warmth enveloped him. The dam he had built to keep everything in, to keep the truth buried, cracked wide open. He leaned into her, his head resting against her shoulder, his arms clinging to her like a lifeline.

And then, the tears came. Silent, shaking tears wracked his body as he buried his face into her neck. He couldn't stop them. He didn't want to.

Katherine held him tighter, her tears falling as she whispered soothing words, her hand running through his hair. She didn't ask any more questions, and she didn't press him for details. She knew that whatever it was, it was too heavy to share right now.

"I'm here," she murmured, her voice breaking. "I'm here, Doug. Whatever it is... we'll get through it. Together."

They stayed like that for what felt like hours, holding each other, crying together, the weight of the world pressing down on them. And though Doug couldn't bring himself to tell her what had happened, her presence was enough at that moment.

For now, the pain and the guilt could wait. All that mattered was the warmth of her arms, the steady beat of her heart, and the small, fragile hope that maybe—just maybe—they could survive this darkness together.

CHAPTER 19

The late Bishop Ed and Lady Eleanor Harrington's family home was always warm and inviting, the rich aroma of roasted turkey and cinnamon wafting through the air as Eleanor stood at the head of the long dining table. The chandelier above cast a soft glow, illuminating the carefully laid-out Thanksgiving feast that stretched across the polished wood. A cadre of servers moved around the table, making sure plates overflowed with sweet potatoes, dressing, cranberry sauce, and freshly baked rolls surrounding the massive turkey, its golden skin glistening. Family heirloom china and silverware sparkled under the light, and each place setting was perfectly arranged, as though Eleanor had been planning this dinner for weeks.

The soft murmur of conversation filled the room, but there was an undercurrent of tension. The Harringtons, though together, had been divided in ways that stretched far beyond the distance between their seats. William sat beside his wife, JoAnn, across from Constance, his eyes lingering on his phone more than the food. Constance, ever the perfectionist, kept her hands neatly folded in her lap, her expression unreadable as she occasionally glanced toward Doug, who sat at the far end of the table.

Pastor Doug, who had barely touched his plate, looked tired—worn, as though the weight of the family's legacy sat heavily on his shoulders. And then there was Katherine, his wife, seated beside him, her face guarded but serene.

Eleanor watched them all in silence, her heart heavy with the unspoken words that had festered far too long. The family she had once prided herself on, which had stood strong under the church's banner, was shattered like broken glass. And for the first time, she was ready to admit that much of that was her fault.

Clearing her throat softly, Eleanor tapped her glass with a silver spoon, the delicate sound cutting through the chatter. The room fell silent, all eyes turning toward her. She looked down at the turkey for a moment, gathering herself, then raised her gaze to meet each of her children's eyes.

"I wanted to take a moment," Eleanor began, her voice steady but soft, "to say something that's long overdue."

She saw the flicker of confusion in William's eyes, the slight narrowing of Constance's brow. On the other hand, Doug looked at her intently as though he had been waiting for this moment without realizing it was finally here.

Katherine's expression remained calm, but there was subtle tension in how she held herself, her hand resting on Doug's arm.

On the other hand, JoAnn always seemed to add a sense of uncanny curiosity to the family because her marriage to William was good as long as she and their kids were financially secure.

Eleanor clasped her hands in front of her. What she was about to say loomed heavy on her conscience.

"I know I haven't always been the mother you needed me to be," she continued, her voice growing somber. "And for that, I owe each of you an apology, *I am sorry*. When your father was alive, I wasn't...I wasn't as strong as I should have been. I sat quietly in the background, as he led this family and led the church, and in doing so, I am also to blame for many of his choices that hurt all of us." Her eyes shifted toward Doug, her youngest, and she felt the sharp sting of regret in her heart. "I didn't stand up when I should have. I didn't protect you all the way a mother should."

A profound silence followed her words, the room heavy with emotion. William looked down at his hands, then glanced at his wife with an unreadable expression. Constance's lips pressed together, her composure cracking just slightly. Doug's gaze remained locked on his mother, his jaw tight but his eyes soft, filled with pain and understanding. Katherine's face, though guarded, seemed to soften as she listened.

Eleanor continued, her voice trembling now. "I am sorry... for the years I spent standing on the sidelines, letting things happen because I thought it was my duty as a pastor's wife to be quiet and submissive. I was wrong in many ways for the pain that my silence caused for the suffering you all endured."

She turned to Katherine, the woman who had married into their family and been met with resistance, judgment, and disapproval—most of it from Eleanor herself. Katherine's eyes met hers, cautious but unwavering.

"Katherine," Eleanor said, her voice softening further. "I owe you the biggest apology of all. I know I haven't been kind to you. I know I made you feel like an outsider when you deserved nothing but love and acceptance from this family. You've stood by Doug through everything, and I... I made that harder for you. For that, I'm truly sorry."

Katherine blinked, visibly taken aback by the words, her lips parting slightly in surprise. She didn't speak, but the tension in her shoulders seemed to ease just a fraction. Doug glanced at his wife, his hand moving to cover hers, offering silent support as Eleanor continued.

"JoAnn," as she gazed in her direction. "I am sorry. You deserved more from me for what you experienced, and I take full accountability for the pain you have carried all these years. I love you and my grandchildren. I promise to be more present in your life."

"I don't expect things to change overnight," Eleanor said, looking around the table again. "But I want you all to know that I intend to be a better role model—for you, the grandchildren, and this family. I've spent too many years hiding behind religious traditions and reputation. It's time for me to stand up and make amends with myself."

The room remained silent, her children watching her with expressions that ranged from cautious to stunned. Eleanor took a deep breath, knowing that this next part was perhaps the most important.

"And one more thing," she added, her voice growing firmer. "Doug is going to need all of our support going forward. As your mother, I'm telling you now, I expect each of you—William, Constance—to be there for him in whatever way he needs. This family is not what it once was, but Doug is doing his best to lead the church and to carry on the legacy despite everything we've been through. I know it hasn't been easy for him and won't get any easier. But he cannot do it alone."

Constance and William, in synchronized union, looked at Doug and offered supportive head nods.

"I can't speak for everyone here, but I can speak for myself," Eleanor continued. "Seeing Dr. Riggio helped me face some things—a lot of things—I'd suppressed going back to my childhood leading up to my marriage with my husband, Bishop Harrington. I was never a fan of therapy—because of my insecurities, abuse, and secrets, I wanted to keep my issues to myself, hidden—however, I no longer feel that way. I'm beginning to change."

"That said, I require everyone here to continue their sessions with Dr. Riggio. I've already paid her in advance for one year, so you don't have any excuses. Thank you, son, Pastor Doug, for standing in the gap for all of us, including yourself. I've had Harry—my attorney—revise my will to let you know how serious I am about this. If the good Lord takes me within the next year, he will monitor your visits to Dr. Riggio. If anyone skips an appointment for any reason that doesn't involve you being in the hospital, your inheritance will be reduced by five percent for every missed appointment."

"Five percent, Mama?" William said, clearly bothered by that part of her speech.

In true diva fashion, Eleanor glared at her oldest child and said sternly, "I can tell Harry to change yours to a ten percent deduction for every missed appointment if you want me to."

"No, ma'am," William said and shook his head vigorously.

His siblings laughed.

"I thought you'd see things my way," Eleanor said. She looked at each of her children again, her voice steady and full of quiet resolve. "This family has been through enough division. It's time to unite and rebuild what we've lost as the bible says in Joel 2:25, "*So I will restore to you the years that the swarming locust has eaten, the crawling locust, the consuming locust, And the chewing locust, my great army which I sent among you,*" (NKJV)."

A silence fell over the table, but it wasn't the tense, uncomfortable silence that had hung over them before. It was something different, softer, a moment of reflection and, perhaps, the first step toward healing and, hopefully, heartfelt forgiveness.

Eleanor felt the weight of her words settle over her, but for the first time in a long time, she didn't feel burdened by it. She felt lighter, as though the truth had finally set her free.

Doug's eyes widened slightly at her words, his expression a mixture of surprise and gratitude. When he and his mother made eye contact, he mouthed, "*Thank you.*"

Eleanor winked and mouthed, "*You're welcome.*"

"Now, I think we're all about ready to eat. William, I want you to say the grace."

William looked shocked. "Umm, I can, but I thought Dougie would say grace."

"Dougie is our pastor, but this is my house. And on this day, I want my oldest child to say the family's Thanksgiving grace. Is that a problem?"

"No…no ma'am." William perked up like he'd been zapped with a taser. It was the first time Eleanor placed him in charge of anything, especially something so sacred as leading the family in prayer at Thanksgiving. Even a blind person could see how grateful and moved he was by the gesture.

"Before you say grace, William," Eleanor looked at Pastor Doug, "Dougie, is there anything you'd like to say?"

Pastor Doug took the cue. He rose from his seat first, his eyes glassy with unshed tears. He walked over to his mother and wrapped his arms around her, his grip firm, secure, and full of understanding.

"Before I say anything, I just want to say we love you, Mom," his voice thick with emotion.

"I love you too, son, I love all of you," Eleanor responded while embracing Doug.

The rest of the family stood one by one, moving toward Eleanor, surrounding her in a way they hadn't in years. Katherine lingered for a moment, watching the scene unfold before finally joining them, her hand resting gently on Eleanor's arm.

Eleanor felt hope for herself, her family, and their future for the first time in years.

CHAPTER 20

Pastor Doug stood before the bedroom mirror, adjusting the knot in his tie for what felt like the hundredth time. His hands shook slightly as he tugged at the fabric, trying to get it to sit just right. The deep green tie was supposed to be festive, a nod to the holiday season lingering in the air, but right now, he felt like he was suffocating because it seemed to get tighter and tighter with every tug. His reflection stared back at him—tired, uncertain, and not at all like the confident man of God he was expected to be. He felt drained, his mind filled with conflicting emotions and unanswered questions. He had barely slept, his thoughts running wild in the dead of night, replaying everything that had happened over the past week: Clarence's death, Gutter's arrest, family issues, and the stress of the church…it was all overwhelming.

"Doug, you okay?" Katherine's voice broke through his thoughts, soft and concerned.

She stood in the doorway, dressed for church in a simple but elegant navy dress, her eyes full of the understanding that only she could give. She had seen him like this before, on days when the pressure of the pulpit seemed too much, but this time felt different. This time, the burden was heavier.

Doug swallowed hard, glancing at her through the mirror.

"I'm fine," he said, though his voice didn't carry much conviction. He gave the tie one last tug, but it still didn't feel right—nothing did.

Katherine walked over to him, her heels tapping softly against the hardwood floor. She came up behind him, gently resting her hands on his shoulders, and for a moment, Doug closed his eyes, letting himself lean into the warmth of her touch. Her presence, as always, was calming, grounding him when he felt like he was unraveling.

"You don't have to pretend with me," she whispered, her voice low and steady. "I can see it on your face. You're worried."

Doug exhaled, his breath shaky as he opened his eyes and looked at her in the mirror.

"Worried doesn't even begin to cover it," he admitted quietly. "I feel…I don't know. I just feel off today. Honestly, I don't know what I'm going to preach about. I couldn't think of a sermon topic. I did not hear from the Lord on a word—it feels like a hollow place I am trying to escape from with no way of escape."

"Do you know what that tells me, honey?"

"What is that, Katherine?"

"That tells me, Pastor, God wants you to let the Holy Spirit lead you this morning."

Doug nodded in agreement. He looked in the mirror and watched her stand behind him, peering over his shoulder and straightening the knot in his tie to perfection.

"You are a blessing," he whispered.

She kissed his cheek. "And so are you, love." She playfully smacked his butt. "Now, let's go to church. I wanna hear what the Lord places on your heart. I need a word, and I am praying for you, honey!" She said, smiling as they walked out of the bedroom.

As the congregation buzzed with anxious murmurs, Pastor Doug stepped forward, his presence commanding the room. He raised his hands, palms out, and slowly, the murmurs faded into a reverent silence. With a deep breath, he approached the glass podium and looked out over the sea of faces, eyes wide with anticipation, some glistening with tears.

"Brothers and sisters," he declared, his voice deep and resonant, echoing in the sanctuary as he began. "Today, we stand on the precipice of choice!" His gaze sharpened, intensity radiating from him like heat from a flame. "We are called to confront the darkness that creeps into our hearts and lives, cast aside complacency, and embrace the truth!"

Pastor Doug spoke of sin, redemption, and forgiveness painting vivid images of a world lost in chaos and punctuating his words with fervor. "The fires of judgment are real, my friends! The time is now to awaken our spirits, to cleanse our souls!"

The congregation leaned in, captivated, as he gestured dramatically, his passion igniting their own.

"Do not be lulled into apathy! The enemy is cunning, and we must arm ourselves with faith and righteous anger!"

The room pulsed with energy, the weight of his words pressing against them like a palpable force. He wove a tapestry of urgency with each phrase, calling them to action, conviction, and repentance.

"We all come to God with a past. Would you want to go back in time and have a do-over? That's the world of make-believe."

"Here's a wishful-thinking poem:

I wish there were some wonderful place called the Land of Beginning Again.
Where all of our past mistakes and heartaches.
And all of our poor, selfish grief.
It could be dropped like a shabby old coat at the door
And never be put on again. (-Louisa Tarkington)"

"With God, we don't need a do-over. You would only make the same mistakes, or worse. When the Lord redeems our past, that does not mean he takes away the past. He does not undo the past. He does not ignore the past but redeems it, which is called *the redemptive truth*. In turning our lives over to Him, we must give Him our past by releasing our past pain with all its losses and shame. We must hand it all over to the Lord every moment of disgrace. Every word we wish we could take back, all the broken promises, the loneliness, the dreams that died, the dashed hopes, the broken relationships, our successes and failures, and all the scars of yesterday."

"The Lord gives us peace with the past and leads us to a better future. Philippians 4:7 says, *"And the peace of God, which surpasses all understanding, will guard your hearts and minds in Christ Jesus."* Please don't ignore the harsh parts of the past because they are part of your story. But don't dwell on them either."

The congregation showered Pastor Doug with encouragement.

"Amen!"

"Preach, Pastor."

And "Praise God!" were all he could hear from the pulpit.

Pastor Doug began to share a parable. "When I sit down with families in preparation for a funeral, at least 75% of the time, something like this happens: The family meets me, and because of my personality and position as a Pastor, most of the time, they immediately trust me. The family wants to tell me a story of a person they loved. The family starts talking. Often, one of the family members will say something not so flattering about the person, such as they were beautiful and loved by everyone, or sometimes have severe issues like unfaithfulness, or they were on drugs and had no church home."

"On more than one occasion, I would take a risk and say, "They had a problem with alcohol, didn't they?" and an incredible sense of relief could be felt once the words were spoken. I hear a lot of dark secrets that are never spoken publicly. As the family starts to talk, they pause and look at me sheepishly and realize what they've just said. What follows is something like, 'Now, you are not going to say that.'"

"I assure the family that I will focus during the funeral on when the person was at their best. I tell them it is essential not to paint a picture of the person that's not true, but that does not mean I have to dwell on the negative either. Sometimes, the family wants an entire negative aspect erased. As the eulogist, my job as a storyteller is to tell an honest story, not ignoring the past but not dwelling on it. The dead is gone, I want to help the attendees of the funeral through my message."

"I am far from perfect, church, and I don't mean my funeral eulogies to be the ultimate example of God's redemption of the past, but it's the best I can do to try and understand how God sees our pasts. God knows us, but somehow, He sees the best in us. He sees our character emerge through our wrongdoings because He knows our beginning and everything in between our lives."

"Let's turn to 2 Corinthians 7:5-16 (NKJV). My sermon topic today is The Redemptive Truth: *Releasing our Past Pain.*"

"The text highlighted today is (v.9), "*Now I rejoice, not that you were made sorry, but that your sorrow led to repentance. For you were made sorry in a godly manner that you might suffer loss from us in nothing.*" As I read today's scripture, Paul is alluding to past conflicts... "*we were harassed at every turn – conflicts on the outside, fears within.*" Paul refers to the hurt he has caused the people of Corinth, "*I see that my letter hurt you...*" Paul does not criticize the Corinthians; he does not try to get even or defend himself, but rather, he says, *Let God redeem our relationship; let us draw closer to the Lord by trusting in him.*"

"Paul brings out the whole idea, not of ignoring the past, but focusing on what is good from the past, "*when we were at our best.*" We all know people who major on everything wrong, complain about the past, and lament that which was hurtful, and they say the same thing over and over and over, seemingly never moving on. Too many folks are stuck in the past. Redeeming the past means finding what is right and what is good."

"If anything is excellent or praiseworthy, think about such things. Redeeming the past means looking for God among us and how God has shaped our character. I like how one person defined history: "the place where character and circumstance met." Redeeming the past starts with understanding the nature of God's promises in this life: God's promise is not to give you a perfect, stress-free life, but instead, God promises to help you through (Read v. 10). Not only to make it through but shape you into a more faithful person. If you are living with tension in your life, or if your life is turned upside down because of a broken relationship, my prayer for you is that you make it through and that you make it through as a stronger person of faith."

"Being a Christian does not mean a pain-free life! Years ago, I was impressed by a book by Dave Draveki, an MLB pitcher who lost an arm to cancer. In his book, Dave Draveki said, "In America, we tend to pray for healing, for God to take away the pain, to overcome the problems. In other countries, people pray, "Lord, help me endure." Christians are not immune from broken relationships. A broken relationship is always because something went wrong. The relationship was once good, and something happened to cause tension, perhaps a bad decision or a betrayal. God does not say, "I will undo your past."

"Everyone has a past. God's promise is, *"I will redeem your past. I will give you peace. I will*

shape your character to be a stronger person of faith." I see that in our scripture reading with Paul and the Corinthian church. Yes, things happened, and we had problems, but look at the strength that has emerged. God was there through it all, and He will make us stronger because of it."

"How does God redeem your past? Start by looking for the silver lining. In v 5-6, Paul alludes to all his difficulties, but in v. 7, he speaks of *a measure of joy*. But Paul goes deeper than just finding the silver lining or trying to put a happy face on the past. That's only the beginning, and there is so much more."

"Again, how does God redeem your past? (v. 9) Look for the power of God amid the tension of your past and ask for forgiveness. Repentance means learning from your life's mistakes and sins and turning your life around. It's not a hard concept. Establish better patterns, live with better attitudes, and make better choices. That's the power of God. That's the hope of a better tomorrow. The best thing about getting older is that I have more of life to look back on and see God's hand in my life."

"Understand the difference between Godly and worldly sorrow. (v. 10) The difference is simple: when you lament the past, does it drive you to God? World sorrow is hollow; it has no roots, object, or way out. Godly sorrow throws your emotions, trust, and faith into God's arms. (v. 10) speaks of sorrow without repentance, meaning nothing ever changes, no hope, no future, no confidence that anything will ever change. The NLT says, "For God can use sorrow in our lives to help us turn away from sin and seek salvation. We will never regret that kind of sorrow. But sorrow without repentance is the kind that results in death."

"God promises you a better life of peace and salvation, not by undoing your past, not by giving you a perfect stress-free life with everyone getting along at all times, but by

focusing on that which was right, by opening your eyes to see his presence during the good and the bad, by giving you the gift of forgiveness as you repent of your past sins, attitudes, and patterns and use the past to grow in your faith. There is no statute of limitations on repentance."

"Redeeming your past does not mean the past changes, but rather, when you look at your past

with the eyes of faith, the power of God emerges, repentance sets you on a path right living (i.e., righteousness), and joy emerges because of what the Lord has done for you. How do you restore a broken relationship? Let God redeem you first. You will appear as a stronger person of faith!"

"In closing, as your Pastor, I need to repent and apologize to you, my church, my family, and myself. I am not proud of certain things I have done. Lives have been ruined, people hurt, trauma inflicted, and power misused. The mantle of a Pastor is heavy to carry, and in our humanity, we all are subject to falling short of God's Glory—pressure bursts the pipe when it is full, and since becoming your Pastor, the pipe has been full."

"It will behoove me to stand before you today without confessing my convictions and repenting for my wrongdoings. No, church, all things cannot be discussed across the pulpit, but know that I am sincerely convicted of my wrongdoings of all things connected to our church, congregation, and my life. I pray and ask that you will forgive me in your *unknowing* as I strive to forgive myself in my *knowing*."

"We are all subject to the sins of this world! I am sorry, church." He said humbly.

"Now, let us stand for the benediction."

All members attending the morning service stood clapping their hands and saying Amen in unison.

As Pastor Doug stood and looked at the congregation, he silently thanked God for trusting, choosing, and forgiving him despite his many life failures and shortcomings.

He then extended his hand and proclaimed the closing benediction.

"Now to Him who is able to establish you according to my gospel and the preaching of Jesus Christ, according to the revelation of the mystery kept secret since the world began but now made manifest, and by the prophetic Scriptures made known to all nations, according to the commandment of the everlasting God, for obedience to the faith—to God, alone wise, be glory through Jesus Christ forever. *(Romans16:25-27) NKJV*

May the strength of God sustain us; may the power of God preserve us; may the hands of God protect us; may the way of God direct us; may the love of God go with us this day and forever. *Amen.*"

Pastor Douglas Harrington, II

THE END

ABOUT
DR. KETRA L. DAVENPORT-KING

Charismatic, energetic, and captivating describe Dr. Ketra's personality. Armed with over 20 years of serving the community, Dr. Davenport-King is an advocate, speaker, mentor, life skills coach, and philanthropist who has radically impacted the lives of believers under the flagship of her ministry.

Dr. Ketra, a native of Dallas, Texas, received her Bachelor of Arts and Science in Christian Counseling, Master of Arts in Christian Education, and Master of Business Administration from Dallas Baptist University. She earned her Doctorate in Strategic Leadership from Regent University. She has spent much of her life serving people in various capacities. One of her greatest joys is starting Life After Advocacy Group, Inc., in 2004, to help individuals who have been victims of sexual abuse recover and live a healthy life.

Dr. Ketra opened the doors to Rock Dimensional Consulting. Through RDC, she has spent over 20 years coaching, mentoring, and training leaders, developing and educating church ministries, and hosting leadership seminars and workshops. Dr. Ketra is known for her innovative and engaging leadership seminar, The Leadership ReCourse, which was designed to reconnect today's leaders to collaborative leadership. Dr. Ketra wholeheartedly believes, "When you live in a community, there should be a handprint of your work left behind for future generations." She launched the North Vernon Women's Community Bible Study Group to bridge the gap and bring together a diverse group of women to improve the family dynamic in underserved communities.

Her greatest accomplishment is sharing her story in Seeing Beyond the Shattered Glass, a fictional memoir based on her true-life events. She is an award-winning and #1 Best-Selling Author and has received a Christian Literary Henri Award. Dr. Ketra continues to share stories through her writing to aid others in the process of becoming FREE from childhood abuse and trauma. She is confident her books will inspire overcomers of sexual abuse who suffer in silence to find their voice and speak their truth.

Author's contact information

Dr. Ketra L. Davenport-King
AUTHOR | ADVOCATE | CONSULTANT | SPEAKER
P.O. Box 163
Mansfield, TX 76063
info@lifeafterag.org
www.LIFEAFTERAG.org | www.DRKETRA.com